**There was Jack Munroe
with a vase of white rosebuds
cradled in his hands.**

"These are for you, to say thank you. I owe you an apology," Jack said.

"Please, don't worry. It was understandable given the circumstances."

Katherine had to move closer to accept the bouquet, close enough to notice he didn't wear a wedding ring. Not that she should be noticing. Not that she *wanted* to.

"You're generous to say that. Needless to say, I don't take criticism of my daughter very well."

"I wasn't criticizing her. Just trying to make things right. Everyone makes mistakes, especially teenagers."

How could he have gotten it so wrong? The woman wasn't high and mighty, she wasn't righteous and judgmental. She was amazing. And if he stood here one second longer and kept this conversation going, then he was going to make a huge mistake.

Books by Jillian Hart

Love Inspired

*The McKaslin Clan

JILLIAN HART

makes her home in Washington State, where she has lived most of her life. When Jillian is not hard at work on her next story, she loves to read, go to lunch with her friends and spend quiet evenings with her family.

Jillian Hart
Precious Blessings

Steeple
Hill®

Published by Steeple Hill Books™

STEEPLE HILL BOOKS

Steeple
Hill®

ISBN-13: 978-0-373-81297-4
ISBN-10: 0-373-81297-3

PRECIOUS BLESSINGS

www.SteepleHill.com

Printed in U.S.A.

But the fruit of the Spirit is love, joy, peace, patience, kindness, goodness, faithfulness, gentleness and self-control.
—*Galatians* 5:22-23

Chapter One

"Go on, do it." The barely audible whisper skimmed over the tall aisle of displayed greeting cards on the other side of the store.

Ordinarily, there was too much noise in the Corner Christian Book Store to hear a low, private conversation. But with the heavy February snowfall tumbling just outside the Spring Is Coming front window display and the fact that most of the customers had hurried through their shopping and left for home when the snow began falling in earnest, the whispering was almost too loud in the quiet, nearly empty store.

Katherine McKaslin didn't stop her work straightening and restocking the greeting-card display, but she did look around. The last time she'd heard those words whispered in the store, someone had been shoplifting.

Two teenage girls stage right, between the crystals case and the humorous greeting cards. They giggled softly, their heads bobbing together to tell secrets. All Katherine could see of them over the chin-high displays were the tops of their heads. One had a tuft-like hairdo of orange spikes, and her friend had blond hair streaked with blueberry strands.

Ah, teenage rebellion. It was a stage she'd missed entirely, which was probably why she was thirty-two and still single. She'd always been stuck in the same rut. There was comfort in the familiar.

Whenever she got an impulse to color her hair—not orange or blue—and maybe add a few highlights to her plain blond locks or wear shoes with more than a sensible one-inch heel, it was short-lived. What would her family think? How would she explain it?

They'd probably say, that's not like you, Katherine, what's gotten into you? And so here she was, thirty-two and working in her parents' store, wearing sensible low-heeled shoes and a black blazer, blouse and skirt that suited a conservative businesswoman. Ever since she'd been a teenager, she'd been afraid of making mistakes.

"I'll be back," Spence, her brother, called as

he shrugged into his nicest coat. "Send prayers and positive thoughts."

"Already done."

With a chime of the overhead bell, the door swished shut behind Spence and she was alone on the floor. She swung her gaze back to her work, pressing down serious worries over the store's worsening financial situation. Her stomach tightened with dread, but before she could send a prayer on Spence's behalf, a blur of movement caught her eye.

There, in the corner security mirror, she had a perfect view of the blue-haired girl slipping something inside her oversized purple book bag.

Oh, no. You aren't shoplifting, right? Katherine waited, pulse thumping, hoping against hope the teen was reaching for her cell phone. Or maybe the girl was checking where she'd left her keys. Customers did that all the time.

But even as she searched for other possibilities, Katherine knew gut-level that it was serious. One look in the mirror showed the empty spaces in the crystals case right in front of the door. The door that should have been locked. Sure enough, the blue-haired teenager had just made a colossal mistake.

Go on, kid, put the figurines back. That would be the best outcome for everyone involved, she thought as she crossed the floor calmly to the counter. Give the girls the chance to do the right thing.

It had happened before in situations like this and it could happen again. She stared hard at the top of the girls' heads and wasn't surprised when the blue-haired girl looked up. Katherine couldn't tell the girl's exact expression beneath the layers of mascara, thick black eyeliner and shadow, but she thought she saw a flash of fear before a brittle hardness settled into a cold-eyed stare.

Okay, maybe not the nicest girl on the planet, but she didn't look like the worst, either. And that brief flash of genuine emotion was telling. The girl wasn't well practiced at stealing. Maybe she wasn't a hardened criminal just yet.

"Put them back, please." Maybe the *please* had been a little too polite. That was another one of her problems. "Return the figurines or I'll call the police."

Those hard eyes widened in horror. In a split second both girls dashed around the display case, and raced toward the door.

Big mistake. This was *not* what she wanted. Katherine took off after them, heart heavy, as the detectors went off. The girls flew out onto the sidewalk. Another few seconds and they'd be lost in the thickly falling snow.

Kelly slung open the break room door. "What's wrong?"

"Shoplifters. Call the cops."

Trusting her best employee to make the call, Katherine hurried out into the storm. The blast of the cold January snowstorm struck her like a brick wall. She swiped the wind-driven snow from her face. Which way had they gone?

North, into the storm and in the direction of the high school, judging by the fresh sets of boot prints. The veil of snow thickened, and they were gone from her sight. Right along with about two hundred and fifty dollars in merchandise she suspected.

Great. Katherine dropped to a walk, lost in the swirling snow. It wasn't the financial loss to the store that bothered her. Those girls were on a troubled path. The police were on their way, and it was out of her hands now. Too bad, because she knew how devastating the consequences of a single act could be.

Watch over them, Lord, she prayed. Those girls would need all the help they could get.

"They're on their way," Kelly's voice called through the storm. "Katherine? Are you out here?"

"Yes, thanks, Kelly. Go back inside where it's warm." Too bad her toasty and sensible goose down coat was hanging neatly in the break room closet. She could really use it about now. Her teeth chattered; she was already an icicle. There was no sense chasing after the girls in this cold, not when she had no chance of catching them, since she was probably the slowest runner in the world.

Best to head back inside and wait for the—

A flash of blue shot through the thick veil of snowfall. The police? Were they already here? Talk about a quick response. Lights strobed dully, but the vehicle had stopped somewhere in the middle of the parking lot. Had they caught sight of the girls?

The beam of red and blue faded. Didn't they usually leave those on? She couldn't see a thing, the storm was whipping up into whiteout conditions. Then a girl's voice rose above the wind just up ahead and Katherine rushed toward the sound.

"Hurry, Dad!" One of the girls' voices rose above the wind. "We gotta get outta here *right now*. Uh…cuz we're totally freezing."

Perfect. The dad had come to pick up the girls, and she could fix this right now. Speak with the man responsible for his shoplifting teenager. Not that she liked confrontations, but this had to be done. She wasn't sure what had happened to the police cruiser, but the slam of a door told her she was running out of time. Hurry. She could still catch them.

Suddenly, shadows materialized from the shroud of falling snow. She recognized the shape of a patrol car, the taillights glowing faintly red as it idled in the lot. She had a perfect view of the blue-haired teenager sheltered in the front passenger seat, but she couldn't see the driver.

"Officer?"

No response, but the blue-haired girl's shocked face filled the front passenger window. The vehicle eased forward.

"Officer! Wait!" She couldn't believe her eyes. They were actually getting away? What kind of police were the city hiring? Men who covered up crimes for their daughters?

Oh no you don't, mister. Sometimes it paid to be ultra-organized—although some people might call it slightly compulsive. She whipped her pen and notepad of sticky notes she always carried with her out of her pocket and ran after the car, squinting at the faint license plate numbers. Once she had them safely noted, she huffed to a stop and slipped the note and pen safely into her pocket.

The taillights stopped, barely more than a

faint glow in the thick curtain of snow. Thank goodness, he'd stopped. Now she could straighten this out, even if her chest was knotted up so tight she couldn't breathe. She *really* hated confrontations, but she could handle this.

How on earth should she handle this? If this was the responding officer and he was the father of one or both of the girls, then he was going to be upset, naturally. She didn't like upset men, but then, who did? She took a steadying breath. *Lord, help me find the right way—*

Was it her imagination or were those tail-lights coming closer? Wait, the rear bumper was definitely rushing toward her. She stopped running, but her heel slid forward on the ice. She skated right at the approaching license plate. *He was going to hit her.*

Tires squealed and the vehicle stopped. She thudded against the car, stopping her forward skid with her hands against the end of the trunk. Her knee struck the bumper of the car. Pain shot through her kneecap.

A tall shadow of a man emerged out of the snowfall and loomed over her, as big as a grizzly. "What is your problem, lady? I almost hit you. You can't go running at a moving vehicle. What's wrong with you?"

She opened her mouth but no words came.

He halted, towering above her with what had to be over six foot three inches of brawny, powerful man. His baritone boomed like thunder. "Are you hurt?"

He was kind of scary, and her knees wobbled. She opened her mouth again and to her surprise a word actually came out. "Y-yo." Too bad it was a word that didn't make any sense.

"Do you need help? Detox?"

Maybe it was his judgmental tone or the derisive lift of his upper lip, but her shock melted away like ice under hot water. "Excuse me? I certainly have never needed anything close to detox. When my sales associate called 911 for assistance, this isn't what we had in mind. An officer doesn't usually *help* the perpetrators *escape* the scene of the crime. What kind of cop are you?"

Wow, was she being assertive or what?

"I'm the off-duty kind of officer on his way home after a bad shift. And that means I'm in a horrible mood." He put his hands on his hips, emphasizing both the breadth of his iron shoulders and the shadowed gun holstered at his hip. "Now, why did you run at my vehicle?"

"I was writing down your license-plate

number. I told you. We called in a shoplifting incident."

"You're not in any danger?"

"Well, no. Not since you got out of your car."

If that made a dent in his one-track line of thought, she couldn't see it. He was more shadow and substance in the heavy storm, and the snow didn't touch him.

"Look, I'm a state trooper, not a town cop. This isn't my jurisdiction. Why don't you go back into your little store and wait for the proper authorities to show up. And stay away from moving vehicles. You could have gotten hurt."

Wow, she didn't like condescending, self-important men. And it had been a while since one had made her so angry so fast. "I don't need a big strong man like you to tell me that. What I need is for you to bring your daughters back to my store—"

"Daughter. The other girl isn't mine."

"The blue-haired girl stole two collectible figurines from my store."

"No way, lady."

"Are you listening to me? You just aren't getting this through your head, are you?"

Why me? Jack Munroe swiped the snow from his eyes. He wished he could rub away his exhaustion as easily. He was beat, and he'd reached his tolerance quota for the day. The last thing he needed was a high-and-mighty woman like the one standing before him, all judgmental righteousness. He'd used up his patience for dealing with that kind of woman when he'd been married. "You're not in any danger?"

"No."

"Is anyone else in any danger?"

"Uh…no."

"Did you hurt yourself when you ran into my patrol car?"

"No."

"Fine. I don't know why you're so confused, but I've had a hard day. I'm not going to deal with this nonsense, not right now. I suggest you go back inside before you freeze and wait for the local cops to come take your report."

He watched as the woman reached into her slim skirt pocket. Not for a weapon, no, but a hundred-dollar pen and small notepad. She began writing furiously, pausing to sweep off the fat snowflakes that landed on her dainty pink pad.

Leaning in, she squinted at his chest. She was tall, and in the dusk of the storm, her light hair gleamed like platinum. "Your badge number. Now, your name would be…?"

She didn't look delusional and psychotic, not for a woman who was standing in an arctic storm in a designer suit and glaring up at him like a hungry reporter ready to jot down crucial information on her square pad of sticky notes. She didn't look confused, but efficient and organized.

Maybe that was the clue he'd overlooked. He was just dog-tired. He still couldn't understand why she'd run at his car. She wasn't in danger and she wasn't in trouble. "Look, lady, sorry if I missed something. You need help with some shoplifter?"

"Have you heard a word I've said?"

"I just finished a double shift, lady. I'm dead on my feet."

"I'm sure it's difficult for a father to hear—"

"Don't listen to her, Daddy." Hayden popped out of the car and gave him a wide-eyed Bambi look.

Apparently, she'd forgotten about the shocking things she'd done to her face and her hair. And where did she get those clothes? She looked like a thrift shop had exploded on her. He gaped at his daughter, his little girl, and could not see her beneath the layers of thick makeup. A clown wore less makeup.

"We didn't do anything wrong, honest, Daddy."

It was that uh-oh feeling in his gut that kept him from believing her flat-out. One question drilled through his tiredness. What had he missed? There was clearly some misunderstanding on the part of this store clerk.

The sound of an approaching car and the wan glow of headlamps had him turning to look over the snow berm in the center of the parking lot. Thank heaven above. "There are the local uniforms to your rescue."

And mine, he thought.

"Fine. Are you coming or not?"

"Now why would I do that? Hayden, get back in the car." He meant to take a step back, but it was as if some unseen force held him in place. "You go get the help you obviously need. Good night, ma'am."

Katherine felt her blood pressure soar into the red zone so fast the top of her skull throbbed. "Sure, go ahead and run off. I have the information I need and I'm sure those nice officers will be in contact with you, Trooper...? What's your last name?"

"Munroe. I hope you get this straightened out."

"I will, but I am sorry for your daughter's sake. Sadly, this happens even in a Christian bookstore, and while I'm very faithful and forgiving, a crime is a crime."

Katherine watched the lawman's granite hands fist tight. She felt his gaze sharpen on her like a blade aimed and ready.

"A Christian bookstore?" The trooper's dark brow arched upward. "Hayden, tell me you didn't do this. You didn't shoplift. And not from a Christian bookstore."

There it is, Katherine thought, the possibility cracking through the denial. Good, she'd rather take care of this now, the right way. "Mr. Munroe, I'll see you inside."

She left father and daughter to settle their problems and hurried through the storm to greet the officers climbing out of their cruiser. With every step she took her emotions cooled and she felt the bite of the frigid wind.

And regret.

Chapter Two

This was the last thing he needed right now. Jack swept the white stuff off his hat brim as he watched that bookstore lady disappear into the thick curtain of snow. It had been a long time since he'd disliked a woman so much so fast. He couldn't say why he had such a strong reaction to her—other than the fact that she'd accused his only child of a crime. Not that she was right about it.

No way, he thought, shaking his head, knocking more snow from his brim. Not his Hayden. Her friend, maybe. Now Jan, he'd believe hands down, was a shoplifter. *She* was the problem, a problem he was going to take care of right now.

"Daddy, how can you even think that? I didn't steal whatever she was talking about.

She just wanted to blame us. I don't know why."

Why was it that whenever he looked at his daughter, he looked past the teenager he hardly recognized to the little sweet thing she'd used to be, five years old with her arm around her favorite doll, running to greet him at the door when he came home from work?

You have to face the facts, man. She's not five anymore. The more Jack looked, the more he recognized Heidi in that look. In fact, it troubled him deeply that with every passing day, his daughter was acting out the grief of her mother's death. While time had dulled his sharp grief, it hadn't seemed to do the same for Hayden.

He had to get control of this situation, put his foot down about the kind of friends Hayden had, and maybe get her involved in church activities. He'd been meaning to join a church, but ever since they'd moved to Bozeman six weeks ago, he'd had his hands full juggling crisis after crisis.

Maybe it was time to let a few things fall and take his daughter to church because he had every intention of keeping her on the straight and narrow. She obviously needed it if this was the type of trouble her new friend was into.

"That store lady is just mean, Daddy."

"Get back in the car."

"But Daddy, you don't believe her, do you?" Big innocent eyes stared up at him.

His heart melted. Again, he still saw his sweet little girl. The trouble was, he also saw a strange teenager staring up at him with his Hayden's eyes, while wearing clown makeup and rock-video-star clothes.

A momentary flash of rage turned his vision red, blurring everything. Her doe-eyed expression, the rapid blinking that told him she was lying. Man, was he mad. Yep, Hayden was covering for her friend. And he was going to come down on them both like a ton of bricks.

No more makeup. No more unsuitable clothing. He did not approve of this. Red hazed his vision again. Is this how she went to school? Had she been like this all day? How long would it take to change back into the nice-looking, decent girl he was used to seeing? She had to wash the blue out of her hair. Her appearance had to be a temporary thing so that she could wash the makeup off her face, climb back into the clothes she was supposed to be wearing and he'd never know the difference. If he hadn't stopped by to check on her earlier, he might not have caught this version of his daughter.

Fury wasn't the word. He set the rules and he expected them to be followed. No arguments. No exceptions. No excuses. "Get in the car."

"Good, 'cuz Jan has to be home by four-thirty." She dropped into the front passenger seat and shared a smug look with her friend in the back seat.

Okay, what was up? Whatever it was, his instincts told him he wasn't going to like it. As he folded his lengthy frame behind the wheel, he already knew what he had to do. He had to get this straightened out fast.

"Did you see her shoes?" Jan asked Hayden. "I think those shoes went out of fashion in 1942."

Hayden giggled. "And did you see her skirt? She could be a nun in that skirt."

Okay, he was seeing red again. "Enough. Show some respect. Now I want you to apologize to the store lady and give back whatever it was that you stole from her." He caught Jan's gaze in the mirror as he negotiated through the parking lot. "Got it? Or you'll be in more trouble than you know what to do with. I'll make sure of it."

"It'd be hard to do, since I didn't steal."

"It's true, Daddy. She didn't take anything."

Lord, I'm gonna need a little help here. He

parked next to the townie's patrol car in front of a lit storefront. Welcome to the Corner Christian Bookstore was written in tasteful black script across the double glass doors. The troubled feeling in his gut went from a squall to a full-out hurricane.

"Daddy, you can't stop here. You said we were going to take Jan home."

"That's not what I said."

"You don't want Jan to get into trouble with her mom."

Where had his sweet little girl gone? He stared in shock at the stranger in his passenger seat, and saw the same look his wife gave when she was annoyed. Whatever was going on, he planned to nip it in the bud.

He killed the engine. "You girls are going to do the right thing."

"What right thing?" Hayden acted as if she didn't have the slightest clue what he was talking about.

He couldn't believe she'd do something so wrong as to shoplift. It was out of the question. She knew better. He'd raised her better than that. Even though he could plainly see her unsuitable clothes and makeup, he had to cling to that truth. He couldn't take it if he lost Hayden the way he'd lost his wife.

He studied Jan in the rearview mirror. Yep, there was a flash of anxiety stark on her face. So, it was just like he figured. *She* was the problem. Relief coursed through him. "You girls bring your book bags and come with me. We'll get this straightened out with the book-store lady."

"But I'll be late gettin' home," Jan piped up.

He wasn't fooled; he could sense the fear amping up a notch. "Don't you worry. I'll talk to your mom if she has a problem. This won't take more than a few minutes. Now march."

He figured being late home was about to be the least of Jan's problems.

The late-February storm hit him like the dead of winter. He hadn't acclimated yet to this much colder climate. It hadn't helped that he'd been out in this weather all night. As a new member to the state's ranks, he'd pulled swing shift and would be doing that for the next year at least, before he could hope to move to a day shift. He was exhausted, but he didn't mind working nights or in this bitter cold, not when he considered how good this move was for his daughter.

How good this move was *going* to be, he corrected, once she found a few better friends. Forget Phoenix's heat and sun. What mattered was keeping his daughter growing up the right way.

"Hayden, what are you doing? Go back and get your book bag."

"But Daddy—"

"Do it."

She heaved a dramatic sigh and trudged back to the cruiser. He kept one eye on Jan, who was frowning into the store window. The girl was obviously watching the store lady in her sensible shoes. Jan could take some lessons in sensible attire.

"Hayden, what are you doing?"

"Nothing, Daddy."

"Are you trying to take something out of your book bag?"

"Just looking for my lip gloss."

"Forget it. Close the door. Come on." First things first. He'd deal with this situation, *then* the makeup.

Hayden slung the strap over her shoulder and marched right past him. She and Jan fell into stride side by side, sharing a look he couldn't name.

He followed them to the door. The trouble was that Hayden was choosing the same sort of friends she'd had back in Arizona. Well, he'd fix that right now. Sure of the outcome, he motioned for the girls to go in ahead of him, not at all surprised when the alarm clanged like an air-raid siren. Both girls jumped, and he watched Jan's chin shoot up in sheer rebellion.

Guilty, he figured. He watched his daughter's head hang and thought, good. Maybe she'd see the kind of girl Jan was.

To his direct left he spotted the pair of local law enforcement boys standing at the checkout counter along with *that* woman. All three had turned at the sound of the alarm, which fell silent again.

So, they'd been filling a report? It looked like Jan had just landed herself in some trouble. He was sorry for that, but maybe there was a silver thread in this. At least it would be a lesson for his little girl. "Hand the officers your bag, Jan."

"That's like so totally not fair. What are you, like a crooked cop?"

"Zip it." And just where had Jan gotten that attitude? His gaze arrowed to his daughter, who was gazing innocently at the ceiling. Her sweetheart face was flushed bright red. He couldn't imagine how any amount of embarrassment could show through so much make-up.

"Do, it Jan. Hey, ma'am—" He motioned to *that* woman stalking toward him. "Here's your culprit. Satisfied?"

"Hardly."

As she snapped closer on those shapely heels, he saw her for the first time in full light. Snow still melted in the liquid sunshine of her long, sleek hair, which framed her intelligent, oval face. He was helpless to look away from her.

She wasn't pretty. No, that was too plain a word. She wasn't beautiful, that was too ordinary. He didn't want to like this woman, but he did appreciate the natural look of lush lashes over her big, violet-blue eyes.

Her perfect nose had an elegant slope and her high delicate cheekbones were classic, not that he ought to be noticing. She had a soft mouth with tiny smile lines in the corners, as if she laughed often. Her chin, dainty and finely cut, complemented her face to perfection.

No, she wasn't beautiful, she was more than that. Striking, that's what she was. Classic. She was a real impressive lady, and she dressed the part in a tailored jacket, blouse and skirt. Lovely.

Not that he was noticing. Merely an observation.

He had a hard time being civil to a woman who had wrongly accused his little girl. Or to the teenager who had actually done the stealing.

"I'm going home. Later, Hayden," Jan said, then marched right back the way she came.

Not his problem, he thought as the door swung shut behind her. He'd delivered the true culprit. It was up to the local boys to deal with Jan. He shot a hard look at that woman, who was glaring up at him as if he were personally responsible.

"I'm taking my daughter home." He laid one hand on Hayden's shoulder to steer her back through the detectors.

"Excuse me, Mr. Munroe?"

"You're testing my patience, lady." He turned on his heel. Behind her the two officers looked less than certain. What was their problem? "Look, I've been on shift since six o'clock last night. It's now 3:56 p.m."

"I'm aware of the time, Mr. Munroe."

"There was a semi jackknifed on the interstate just out of the city limits, and I spent most of the night and half the day seeing to the clean-up and the investigation. I'm dead on my feet." He looked past the unhappy woman to the uniforms standing beside her. "I'd appreciate it if you boys would wait to give me a call if you need a statement."

Sheer exhaustion had him steering his Hayden back toward the door.

"Uh, Mr. Munroe?" That woman—that extraordinarily annoying woman—called after him. "Wait—"

He kept going. Maybe by tomorrow he would have cooled down enough to offer *that* woman the apology he probably owed her for his snarky mood. Even if she *had* wrongly accused his daughter.

A deafening claxon squealed right in his ear. He saw the guilty look sneak across his little girl's face and still his denial remained. Not his Hayden. Maybe Jan had put the stolen items in Hayden's bag. Maybe they had accidentally fallen off the shelf and into her bag.

He was desperate and he knew it, but it simply couldn't be true. His daughter? His Hayden had said she didn't do it. She'd lied, too. Anger began to huff up with each strangled breath.

"Daddy, I can explain. I didn't know." She looked at him desperately with a helpless gesture and those wide innocent eyes.

He *wanted* to believe her. Except his common sense had kicked in and, fueled with the rage, he was trembling with temper. Careful, controlled, he gritted his teeth to hold back the overwhelming urge to shout, a natural reaction to a teenager's misbehavior. "Take what you stole out of your bag and give it back."

"But, Daddy, I—"

"You heard me. Do it."

Hayden gave a put-upon sigh but bowed her head and started digging through her things. It took all his effort and a quick prayer for self-control to stand there and not explode like a lit keg of ten-year-old dynamite.

One look at that woman had him praying for an extra dose of control. Overwhelming irritation jabbed deep into his chest. Probably from lack of sleep, sure, but the bookstore lady agitated him. To make matters worse she held out her slender hand, palm up, to receive a very expensive-looking cut-crystal figurine.

"Thank you," she said in that prim voice of hers. "Now I want the other one."

"There's only one." Hayden attempted the wide-eyed look again.

Katherine shook her head, her gaze locking on the teenage girl's. "The lamb figurine has a security strip, too. What do you think is going to happen when you turn around and head back out the door?"

"Oh. Okay."

The big man's jaw dropped as his daughter's innocent expression faded. She dug out a second figurine.

It was a sad thing to see a man lose belief in

his child's innocence, Katherine thought. The big hulk of a state trooper puffed up like a weightlifter getting ready to set an Olympic record. His hands fisted and his hard, masculine mouth drew downward in a heartbreaking frown. The tarnished glint of shock in his handsome brown eyes ought to have made a sensible teenager feel shame and vow never to disappoint her dad like that again.

But not this girl. She tossed her hair as she handed back the figurine. "Have it. I didn't want it anyway."

"Well, you took it," Katherine said with care. "And giving these things back doesn't change the fact that you stole them in the first place."

"Miss McKaslin," one of the local officers shouldered in. "We can handle it from here."

"You're pressing charges?" Jack Munroe raised his fists to his forehead as if his skull was about to blow.

Poor man. She felt sorry for him, but it didn't change the facts. "You know the consequences of shoplifting. Does your daughter?"

"Does it need to come to that?" His hands dropped away, revealing stark sadness etched into the planes of his face. He radiated responsibility. "Believe me, I'll set her straight.

There's no need to take this any further. Please."

She didn't know what to do with his obvious sincerity. He seemed invincible iron, and his gaze meeting hers shone with hard honesty. She could sense his hurt like cold in a winter wind. He was a good man, she could see it.

It was the girl she had to consider, who glared through her thick, spiky mascara-coated lashes with a ha-ha attitude.

Katherine quietly placed the crystal lamb in her blazer pocket along with the shepherd and considered her options. She didn't doubt that Jack Munroe had been up all night working, just as he'd said. Dark exhaustion bruised the skin beneath his eyes, and she wagered that this mighty mountain of a man never did anything that was short of upright and honest his entire life. Pressing charges would hurt him more than the girl.

"She returned the items." He managed to unclench his jaw enough to speak.

"Only when she was caught. If you hadn't brought her back here, she never would have returned the figurines. She's not truly sorry, and that's my concern. This could happen again in another store."

"Lady, I'm gonna ask you." He swiped a

hand over his eyes, a gesture of holding back his temper or one of fatigue, or both. "Please. Let me handle this."

"Then what do you suggest?"

"I don't know." He swung around to glare hard at his daughter, who shrank at his look and finally hung her head in shame.

Maybe not such a tough girl—yet. Katherine folded her arms over her chest, already caring about the girl's welfare. She was a softy, as her brother was always accusing. And it was true. She wasn't worried about the figurines. What worried her was this girl with one foot on a path that could only lead to more trouble. "I'll require restitution."

"How much?" Jack reached for his wallet but stopped as Katherine shook her head.

"No, I'm not talking about money. I want volunteer work."

Jack's head pounded worse as Hayden let out a bellow.

"No way. Daddy, I'm not working for free in this…this *store*. Dad, you can use my allowance money—"

"It's volunteer work," Miss McKaslin interrupted evenly. "The local churches have a united charity, and they always need reliable help. There are a lot of teenagers from the youth groups involved at the free supper kitchen and the shelters. Maybe she could put in, what, sixteen hours of work? That's roughly the value of the figurines. And she'll make some good friends there, I'm sure."

Youth-group kids? That caught his attention. A very reasonable solution. But what cinched it was the belligerent cock of his daughter's jaw.

"I won't do it, Daddy. I'm not gonna waste my time with a bunch of losers and homeless people."

By the Grace of God, he thought. He'd sheltered her too much, he could see that painfully and—maybe, just maybe—spoiled her a little. But how could he have not?

She had no idea about the world he worked in every day. The one where bad things happened to good people, where sometimes the world's harshness could break a spirit, and compassion and doing the right thing held immeasurable value.

It was time for his girl to grow up a little. "We'll take your suggestion, Miss McKaslin."

"Call me Katherine, please. I'll have one of the coordinators call you." She smiled, and tension drained out of her slender shoulders, squared so stubbornly under her tailored blazer.

Even though he didn't like her, he had to

admit she had class. And the smile she extended to Hayden wasn't triumphant, but compassionate, and that impressed him, too. So he couldn't like the woman for accusing his girl, even if she had been right, but he appreciated what she'd done. And handing him the opportunity of forcing his daughter to get involved with a youth group was just what he'd needed.

Being new to town and settling into a house and a job had taken a lot of his energy. Other priorities had been shoved aside. But no more. Resigned, he accepted the pen and notepad Katherine had taken from her pocket and handed to him.

As he jotted down his home number, he couldn't help noticing the subtle hint of her perfume, something light and tasteful. He couldn't say why his hand shook a little as he returned the pen and notepad.

Probably because he was working on twenty hours without sleep. That was it. "Thank you."

Katherine wasn't sure what to say to a father who had a big challenge on his hands. But despite her attitude, she was certain that his daughter was a good kid down deep. "Good luck."

"You say that like you think I'm going to need it," he said.

"I'm sure things will be smooth sailing for you from here. Hayden, you're going to like Marin. She's a cool youth pastor."

"I don't *think* so." The girl rolled her eyes and gave her shank of blue hair a toss behind her shoulder and headed back through the detectors. "C'mon, Daddy, let's get out of here."

For an instant, Jack Munroe looked like he feared his daughter would set off the alarm again. His wide, linebacker's shoulders looked as rigid as granite, as if he carried a heavy burden on them. Once they were through the sensors without an alarm, a visible wave of relief passed over his handsome features.

Yep, he was going to need more than good luck. She would put him on her prayer list tonight.

She turned to thank the town officers, who were already on their way out.

Kelly looked up from the book she was reading at the register. "Are you okay? You don't look okay."

"I'm fine. Now that it's quieted back down, I don't think we're going to see a lot of business with this storm. Did you want to go home? The roads are only going to get worse."

"But then you'll be here alone."

"I'm going to close down early. Don't you worry about me. Just drive safely, okay?"

"Thanks, Katherine." Kelly gathered up her college textbooks and headed toward the back.

Alone. Katherine wrapped her arms around her middle. She was getting real used to being alone. Lights flashed on and glared in the front window—the headlights of the state trooper's cruiser. He was talking to the daughter. She could barely make them out through the thickly falling snow.

Maybe it was the ghosts of old memories rising up, or seeing those girls, teenage girls, and remembering what was best not thought about, but she hurt.

All it took was one wrong move, even well-intentioned, and look how far-reaching the consequences. This was her life, she thought. She turned her back on father and daughter and went back to restocking.

Turned her back on memories that, felt anew, would keep her up most of the night.

Chapter Three

"Thanks, Pastor. You have a good afternoon, now." Jack hung up the phone in the quiet of his home office. The empty house echoed around him as he turned in his chair and stared out the window.

A cold winter's landscape met his gaze through the picture window that faced the rugged range of the Montana Rockies, spanning the entire length of the horizon. The ice-capped peaks jutting against a white-gray sky were breathtaking and a change from Phoenix's low camelbacks, which he'd seen all of his life. This Montana landscape wasn't too hard on the eyes, but snow covered everything from the distant mountaintops to the shrubs outside the window. Miles and miles of snow.

Too much snow. Worse, a thick cloud layer

was building across the entire dome of the sky. Just his luck that another six to eight inches were forecast to start falling by sundown. And if it did, then he could kiss his night goodbye.

He better put calling Mrs. Garcia on his to-do list. The sixty-something housekeeper stayed over in the guest room on the nights he worked in order to keep an eye on Hayden. He scribbled *Mrs. Garcia* on line ten, right below the reminder to call the lady from the Christian bookstore.

Miss Katherine McKaslin. He didn't know what to think of her. He owed her. He didn't like her, but he'd behaved badly last night. Yep, that's the way it went. He always wound up coming across like a jerk whenever he was around a single woman. Which worked out just fine, he guessed, since he'd never been more than undecided when it came to the idea of marrying again.

This little shoplifting incident might have a serious silver lining—and that was the youth pastor he'd just spoken to. A friend of *Miss* McKaslin's.

Why couldn't he get her out of his mind? She was tall, slim, proper and lovely, *definitely* lovely. He didn't want to like her. Besides, remembering how angry he'd been over her accusing Hayden—and then her being right about Hayden—was something he was never going to get past.

Not that he wanted to get past it.

Still, it wasn't like he could forget the sympathetic look she'd given Hayden. Sympathetic, when Katherine had the right to be angry, or worse.

You owe her, man. And you know it.

His little girl could have found herself in juvenile detention if Katherine McKaslin had been unforgiving. But instead, the uptight, high-and-mighty shop lady had been nothing of the sort. Her kindness had handed him the best break he'd had in a while. The pastor he'd spoken to on the phone sounded like just the sort of help his little girl needed.

And that brand of decency was hard come by in this world.

By the time the first airy flakes of snow began to fall, he knew what he had to do.

In the quiet of the bookstore, Katherine leaned against the doorjamb to her brother's office and tried to make sense of the male brain. "The dangerous winter storm warning isn't just speculation. It's fact. Have you looked out the window?"

"It's a few flakes. Big deal."

"It's a perfect time to close the store, *before* the blizzard hits. Right?"

"What do we do about the customers who stop by later, depending on us to be open for them? I can't be here. I've got a meeting at the church." Decked out in his best suit, white shirt and tie, Spence gave his computer keyboard a few more taps. The printer in the corner started spitting and clattering. "We can't disappoint our customers. It's not good for business."

"Fine, I'll send everyone home and I'll stay."

"Alone? Like you did last night? You know I don't approve of that. It's not a safe world."

"True, but I'm a capable adult who can take care of herself." Really, she knew her brother cared, but there was only one harder-headed man on this earth, and that was their father, of course. Both of them could test a girl's patience without the slightest effort. "Go to your meeting."

"I can't go if you're going to be here alone."

"Then we close now." Katherine watched her big brother wrestle with that. "I'm going to go out onto the floor. Do you need anything before I go?"

"No. This spreadsheet you did for me is great." Spence straightened his paisley tie as he rose from his leather chair. "I think they'll be pleased."

"Good." She figured that was as close to an okay on closing the store early as she would get. "Drive carefully out there."

She left her brother stewing over his financial worries and the lost revenue of closing early— as if anyone would be out shopping with the current weather warnings. Poor Spence. He took his responsibilities so seriously. Too seriously.

"Hey, kiddo." She cornered the fiction aisle, where her younger sister was shelving books. "You need help with that cart?"

"Sure. You know what the Bible says, two can accomplish more than twice as much as one." Ava straightened from her work with a wink. "You don't look busy."

"You know me, I never work."

"I know. It's terrible. You know what everyone says? That lazy Katherine. Next they'll be commenting on that wild outfit." Ava laughed, a light, easy trill.

"Aren't you funny?" Okay, so she wasn't a fashion plate. Katherine glanced at the black cable turtleneck sweater and her favorite pair of black wool trousers. Sensible, as always. "There's a minus-ten-degree wind chill outside."

"Hey, I know." Ava chose a volume from the cart and turned to study the shelves. Her outfit of choice today was a smart safari jacket, a lace-edged purple Henley and a pair of jeans tucked into suede boots. She looked like she'd walked off a fashion magazine. "I heard you had a little incident last night."

"The shoplifting? Yeah, but we got the figurines back."

"I wasn't talking about that. I heard a rumor that you caught a certain state trooper's attention."

"It's ridiculous. Who did you hear that from?"

"Nobody. Well, Aubrey and me, we felt compelled to review the security tape. Then Aubrey bumped into Dean getting coffee this morning, you know, one of the responding officers last night?"

"Yeah, yeah." It was a small city. Sometimes hardly more than a small town. "You and that sister of yours—"

"She's your sister, too—"

"—have the *wrong* idea."

"Which is?"

"Trust me. That man can't stand me." That had come across pretty clearly last night. "I don't believe you got that from the tape. He was horrible. He—"

"Yeah, so you didn't really notice him at all, huh?"

"Not at all." Katherine grabbed a half dozen books from the cart and moved down the aisle. "I know what you're doing. You're trying to distract me from the fact that you left the crystals case unlocked."

"My bad." Ava didn't look a bit remorseful, and she wasn't doing a whole lot of shelving either. "So, back to the state trooper. Was his name Jack? Do I have that right?"

Yeah, she had the name right. But she was hard-pressed to explain why it felt like the lining of her rib cage contracted painfully whenever she thought of him. "It isn't like that. He's married, I'm sure. And why aren't you shelving?"

"I'll get to it." Ava sidled close. "I happened to notice he wasn't wearing a wedding ring."

"And this is important because…?"

"I don't want you to give up hope."

Why did that make her ache inside, all the way down to her soul?

Because she had lost hope. Hope of ever finding the right man.

"He's out there, I know it." Ava slid a book into place. "I pray for you finding him every night."

Her soul ached a little more. "I'm afraid

you're wasting your prayers. A lot of men just wouldn't understand…."

There was the past left unsaid between them.

Ava's hand found Katherine's and gently squeezed. "You only need the right man to understand. To see what a great woman you are." Her gaze shot over Katherine's shoulder for a brief moment. "I bet he's on his way to you right now. Maybe, so you won't miss him, the Good Lord will send a sign. You know, like a handsome man bringing white roses."

"What are you talking about?"

"Just telling you I think my prayers are going to be answered. I'm lucky that way, you know." Ava snatched another book from the cart. "I pray, it happens. Right?"

"Almost always. *You* have a serious gift with prayer. But you have to accept that some things aren't meant to be. I have." And talking about it was painful. She slipped a historical romance into place on the middle shelf and straightened the books around it. She liked tidy shelves. Keeping the shelves tidy was something she made a difference at.

Repairing the damage done to her life almost fifteen years ago was something that could never be done. Not even God could change what was past.

The bell over the door chimed. A customer, she wondered, or Spence back from the meeting that was probably cancelled?

"You'd better go see who that is," Ava commented as she laboriously struggled to slip a paperback book onto the shelf, obviously too busy to check on the possible customer.

What was up with her? Katherine glanced around the aisle and the book she held slid from her fingers. As the book hit the floor, the thud sounded just like her heart stuttering in shock. There was Jack Munroe, broad-shouldered and substantial, with a vase of white rosebuds cradled in his big, capable-looking hands.

That Ava. She must have spotted him getting out of his car. Really. "Hello, there. How are things working out with your daughter?"

"Better. She'll be grounded for about the next decade or so. Nothing major." He handed over the roses along with a striking half grin. "These are for you, to say thank you. I owe you an apology. I'm sorry I was such a...well, I can't say it in polite company."

"Please, don't worry. It was understandable given the circumstances."

"You're generous to say that. Needless to say, I don't take criticism of my daughter very well."

"I wasn't criticizing her. Just trying to set things right."

"I know that."

She had to move closer to accept the bouquet, close enough to notice that Ava was right. No wedding ring. She also noticed how the green and gold threads in his dark-brown irises softened the gaze that had seemed so imposing last night. Laugh lines added character to his face.

Not that she should be noticing. Not that she *wanted* to.

Katherine breathed in the sweet old-fashioned roses' scent. It was hard to dislike a man bearing flowers—from both him and Hayden, obviously. "Thank you. This was thoughtful of you."

He smiled, a full-fledged one that made those threads in his eyes glint. Very nice. She snapped away, focusing her energy on setting the vase on the front counter instead of feeling the effects of that smile.

Where was Ava? Katherine had the feeling that her sister, with her matchmaking thoughts, was spying through the book stacks. Really.

Katherine did her best to appear unaffected, because of course, she was. "How is Hayden doing?"

"Mad at me. Mad at you. But I think that's a teenage thing. She's probably angriest at herself."

"Probably."

"I got a hold of your pastor friend this afternoon. She said you'd already called and told her about Hayden wanting to join the youth group's project at the shelter. She didn't know anything about the shoplifting problem."

"I didn't feel like it was my place to tell her. Everyone makes mistakes, especially teenagers."

Her words of compassion struck him like a sucker punch to the chest. His first impression of this woman had been way off base. Out in left field. He didn't know how to tell her that. Didn't know if he should.

"I've been friends with Marin forever. She has all kinds of youth-group activities and projects going on all the time, not just with the shelter. Hayden will love her, I promise."

"I believe you." How had she gotten past his defenses so easily? Jack rubbed the back of his neck, puzzled and, he had to admit, intrigued. "You've done a good thing for my girl. I know you're thinking, *That man and his kid are a mess.* But I've been trying to right this boat for a while. Hayden's a good kid."

"I saw that in her. That she's good, without a doubt."

There it was again, that compassion, lovely and kind. Katherine was a striking woman, but with her heart gentle in her eyes, he felt captivated. A strange emotion dazzled through him, and it felt like first light on a bleak winter's morning, changing everything.

Remember, Jack, you don't like this woman. Correction: you don't *want* to like this woman. He scrubbed his hand over his eyes. What had they been talking about? That's right, Hayden. "She's a real good kid. Used to be. Is. Things haven't been smooth for a long time, but this— this shoplifting thing—is the first serious problem we've had. I don't want you to get the wrong idea."

"Believe me, I'm not casting stones."

"It's a little hard for you not to. She stole from you."

"True. But she wouldn't be the first shoplifting teenager in this store. She won't be the last."

How could he have gotten it so wrong? This woman wasn't high and mighty, she wasn't righteous and judgmental. She was amazing. And if he stood here one second longer and kept this conversation going, then he was going to make a huge mistake. She'd done it again, gotten beneath his defenses. He was just about to open up and talk about his life and the part of himself he kept under tight lock and key.

But opening up just made a man vulnerable. So he had one option, and one option only. Time to get out of Dodge while he could. Time to escape before he started thinking that if and when he tried dating again, he'd look for a woman like this one.

Maybe this one.

Nope, he just couldn't see Katherine saying yes to a date with him. She'd turn him down flat. His life was a mess; he knew it. He was no prize, plenty of women he'd dated had said it.

To save what dignity he had left, he headed out into the wind and storm. It was abrupt, probably came across as rude, but he'd done the best he could.

Once inside his cruiser, as he let the engine warm and the fog clear from the windshield, he could see her inside the store, going about her work. There was something about the way she moved with unconscious grace. The way she stopped to tuck a strand of her light blond hair behind one ear, and it was an utterly feminine gesture.

He missed the gentleness of a woman in his

life. Katherine McKaslin made him remember a time when he hadn't been so isolated. When he'd been a man unjaded by life and believing in love's illusions.

Yep, buddy, it's best to just keep on going.

So he put the car in Reverse, backed away from the curb and didn't stop until the bookstore disappeared from his rearview mirror. Until there was just blinding snow behind him and a long, lonely night's work ahead.

Katherine knew what her sister was going to make of it. The moment the back door swung open, she braced for the worst. She was about to get hit with double barrels.

Aubrey, Ava's twin and mirror image, rushed down the devotionals aisle. "Are those the flowers? You were so totally right, Av. White roses. Talk about classy."

Behind the cash register, Katherine tried to take the kidding with the love it was meant. "Nothing says *thank you* like white roses, don't you think? It's a thank-you, girls, not a sign of romance."

Ava abandoned all pretense of shelving and trotted up to add her two cents. "That's the story she's sticking to—"

"—but we know better," Aubrey finished.

"You should have seen how he was looking at her."

"Like on the tape?"

"More."

The twins nodded together, looking as if they were having a twin moment of shared thoughts.

Katherine grabbed the cash tray and closed the empty drawer. "I hope you two are headed home. The state patrol just closed the highway outside of town."

"The *state patrol.*" Ava's tone held huge significance.

"Exactly. She didn't seem riveted to their bulletins before."

"You two." Her face felt hot. Couldn't they see they were embarrassing her? It wasn't easy being the big sister. No respect. "Go. Shoo. Call me when you get home."

"She just doesn't want to talk about him," Aubrey said to Ava.

"Nope. We've seen this stage before."

"The denial stage?"

"Uh-huh." The twins bobbed their heads together. "Are you sure you don't want us to stay?" they asked in perfect unison.

"I'm sure." She loved her sisters. It was impossible not to. They were dear, even at the ripe old ages of twenty-seven, dressed in similar colors and style, naturally identical in just about every way, from the long sweep of their platinum hair to the lopsided crook of their grins. From the day they'd come home from the hospital, she'd always known they were special. A girl couldn't have more loving and loyal sisters anywhere. "Go. I'll give you twenty minutes to make it home and if I don't hear from you, I'm calling."

"Okay, okay."

"Bye."

The twins walked away together, their voices cheerful and growing faint, and then fainter. The back door closed, and she was alone.

And why did Jack Munroe stay on her mind the entire time she closed up and totaled the day's deposit? Maybe it was the delicate perfume from the tightly closed rosebuds. Maybe it was the big deal the twins had made about the man who was showing simple courtesy by bringing flowers as a thank-you. Either way, she was *not* in denial about liking Jack.

Jack Munroe with his grizzly-bear temper and his rigid-spine stance was a black-and-white kind of man. No gray areas allowed. He was an officer of the law. He spent his work life judging others, finding them guilty of speeding or reckless driving or worse. She'd seen the mortification on his face when he'd admitted what his daughter had done. He was a play-by-the rules kind of man.

She *was* looking for that kind of man, but she would guess that Jack Munroe had never made a major mistake in his life. He might have a blind spot when it came to his daughter, and rightly so, otherwise he didn't look like the kind of man who forgave mistakes easily.

So, that was that.

Chapter Four

"This is lame, Dad. I *won't* do it."

Jack lifted his gaze from the mountainside road long enough to take in the confrontational jut of Hayden's chin and the fury in her cool eyes.

Uh-oh. He knew that look. It was the same one he'd been dealing with for most of the week, ever since he'd hauled her home from Katherine McKaslin's store.

"I won't and you can't make me."

Keep your cool, Jack. Through the haze of falling snow, he negotiated the final curve and spotted the exit for the ski resort. "You'll choose to do this or I'm adding more volunteer time to your sentence."

No answer came, but the fury of her silence increased the temperature in the car by a full ten degrees.

It didn't matter. Nothing could change his mind. He'd decided Hayden was going to join Marin's youth group and participate in every single youth-group activity until he got his good Hayden back. He knew she was hiding *somewhere* behind the sullen belligerence. If he had to devote his day off to that cause, then fine. No sacrifice was too great for his little girl.

I saw that in her. That she's good, without a doubt.

Why did Katherine's words come back to him? He could hear her dulcet, precise tone. Could remember the play of the overhead lights on her straight blond locks, held neatly in place by a sensible barrette over each ear. She'd been understated elegance in her modest black sweater and slacks. Katherine didn't need makeup or high fashion to be lovely.

Eventually Hayden would come to the same conclusion about her own appearance. His ears still rang from the heated argument they'd had over her makeup and shocking fashion statement. She'd been wearing her approved school clothes when she left the house each morning, he'd learned, and then had changed at Jan's house, reversing the process after school.

And you didn't even guess it, man. That's what ate at him the most.

Hayden stared out the window with enough hatred to melt half the snow pack on the mountain peaks. "This is all that awful store lady's fault."

"Miss McKaslin is the reason I didn't have to bail you out."

"Right. I can't believe how wound up everybody got over some lousy figurines. Just chill."

Jack hit the brakes and the Jeep skidded into a parking slot. "What has gotten into you? Do you think if you push me hard enough, I'll move us back to Phoenix? Is that what this is about? Then you're flat wrong, missy."

"I hate this place. I wanna go home."

"This *is* home. If you don't want to like it here, fine. But you *will* do one more week's volunteer work—"

"Dad!"

"Another word, and it'll be two." He waited for the red haze of rage beating dully in his eye sockets to fade. The heartbreak of a disappointed father did not.

Hayden's face had scrunched up in resentment, but at least she held back. It was an effort, he could see that by the hard cinch of her mouth, but she stayed silent. That was an improvement.

Relief cooled some of the anger, but didn't

begin to touch the ache in his heart. "Get your things. Pastor Marin said you kids are meeting for prayer and fellowship in the lodge before the group lesson."

More sullen silence. Hayden whipped her door open and shot out of the car, not so eager to join the youth-group meeting, he figured, but to get away from him. Well, he could handle anything she could dish out because he was her father and he was committed. One hundred thousand percent. He grabbed the keys and climbed out into the bitter weather.

Movement caught his eye. A slender woman with her back to him was ambling away from the parking lot. She was dressed in warm sensible skiwear and carrying an expensive set of skis.

Was that Katherine? Surprise sparked like a new flame in his chest.

No, of course that's not her. His surprise faded to nothing, nothing at all. He wasn't even going to tell himself that he was wishing it was Katherine. With the way he'd been so rude, just abruptly walking away from her, if that *was* her, she would probably be running in the other direction as fast as she could.

The slam of the Jeep's passenger door jarred him out of his thoughts. Hayden glared at him, all zipped and bundled up. "Where do I gotta go?"

"First we'll hit the rental place. Get geared up." He pressed the remote to lock the doors. "With any luck, we'll get you to the lodge so you don't miss a microsecond of the meeting."

"Oh, joy."

Hayden marched off ahead of him and didn't look back.

He had that effect on a lot of females.

Katherine *loved* skiing; the sport had only one flaw, the fact that you had to go back up the mountainside. I'm not afraid of heights, she told herself stubbornly, I'm not afraid of heights.

Okay, she was. She'd never been able to talk herself out of this fear. Nor did the view of the rugged terrain far below her skis as she rode the lift ever look any less horrifying. She did the only thing she could do—squeezed her eyes shut.

"I know something to take your mind off falling to our deaths," Marin said, ever helpful. "Hayden Munroe came to our worship and ski program. She's taking her first lesson with the instructor this very moment."

"That's great." Katherine's initial thought

was for the girl who was heading down a very troubled path. "I know you'll have her feeling better about herself and her life in no time."

Her second thought was, unfortunately, about Jack Munroe. Had he brought Hayden to the lodge? And if so, had he stayed?

Don't think about that, Katherine. You're not interested in him, remember?

"That father of hers is sure something." Marin turned to the other member of their trio squished onto the narrow bench. "Holly, you've got to see this guy. It almost makes you believe in Mr. Right."

Holly gasped. "But you don't believe in Mr. Right."

"True. I've done enough marital counseling in my career to know that he's a myth. Katherine, we're almost at the top. You might want to open your eyes now. I'm absolutely sure that there is no Mr. Right anywhere in existence on this earth. Just Mr. *Almost*-Right."

"And those are few and far between." With a scoot off the bench chair, Katherine landed, skis parallel and knees bent. When she turned to look over her shoulder, Holly and Marin swished to a stop behind her. "Trust me, Jack Munroe isn't anywhere close to being Mr. Almost-Right."

"Wow, did you hear that, Holly?"

"I heard it, Marin. Katherine's in her denial stage."

"What *is* it with everyone? The twins said the same thing. I'm *not* in denial. Really."

"Of course you're not," Holly said in a comforting way, although Katherine wasn't fooled. Not one bit. "So, tell me, is this guy—whoa, buddy!"

"Outta the way! Comin' through!" A man shouted, in sheer panic.

Was it her imagination, or did that sound sort of like Jack Munroe? Katherine hopped out of the way just in time to see a blur speed by. The blur was a black-parka-wearing, wide-shouldered man crouched very low over his skis, his poles held straight in front of him as if he were roasting hot dogs over a campfire.

"That looks like doom on two sticks," Marin commented. "I'd better pray for that man."

"He's going to need it. Oh, he went right through the first turn." Holly cocked her head to listen. "He missed the trees. I didn't hear a crash."

What if that *was* Jack? Katherine kicked off and followed Marin down the trail. She couldn't see anything of the fallen skier. That wasn't a good sign. What if he was hurt?

Lord, please don't let him be hurt.

"Hey, Katherine," Marin called as she led the way. "Do you know who that man reminded me of?"

Yeah, she knew. And she was going to stay in denial about that, too. "A beginning skier who missed the rope tow for the bunny run?"

When they reached the first turn, all they could see was a hole in the snowbank and a single ski sliding crookedly along the trail.

Marin reached the edge first. "Mister, are you alive?"

Katherine *knew* it was him, even before his gruff baritone rang out from the trees.

"Yep. And better yet, nothing's broken."

Katherine's heart skipped five beats as she joined Marin at the edge of the bank. Sure enough, she recognized the man below. Although he was in profile, looking down as he tried to free one of his poles from the branches of an evergreen tree, she already knew that particular man's profile by heart. There was no mistaking the hard-planed, granite face. Or the dark shock of hair tumbling from beneath the black ski cap.

It was him. Her stomach clenched tight before it fell downward, tingling, all the way to her knees. Just the way it felt on the uppermost crest of a roller-coaster ride when suddenly down you plunged. Screaming.

Yeah, it was something like that. "J-Jack?"

He looked up. "Uhh...Katherine McKaslin?"

He said it in the same way someone might say, *Oh, good, there's a person infectious with bubonic plague.* "Do you need help up?"

"No! I can do it just fine. You go ahead and keep right on with your skiing."

"Oh no," Katherine said sweetly "we'll stay and make sure you get up all right."

Great. Jack stared at the three women staring back at him. Humiliation eked into his soul like the icy wind through his coat.

Why does it have to be her, Lord? If he was going to disgrace himself, did it have to be in front of Katherine McKaslin? And why was his bad side showing whenever she was around? "I'm fine. Just getting my snow legs back."

"Is that something like sea legs?"

Jack could tell she was holding back laughter. Mirth glimmered like flecks of amethyst in her deep violet-blue irises. He liked the sparkles in her eyes very much. "I haven't skied since college. I figured it would come back to me."

"I hope you didn't ski like this in college."

His pole came loose from the branches and he gave thanks for that. "Believe it or not, I was a pretty competent skier, but it's taking its own sweet time coming back to me."

"I hope it comes back to you before you hit the next turn."

"Me, too." Jack wondered how she could say that in a kind way, when she had every right to mock him? After all, he'd been a little overconfident in his abilities.

Okay, extremely overconfident. He grabbed one ski and hiked up the snowbank. "I heard that comment you made. The one about the bunny run."

"Sound must really carry on this mountain."

"Don't you know it. Truth is, it was my pride. I didn't feel dignified going down the same run as knee-high kids who could ski like Olympians."

"So you chose the advanced run as an alternative?"

"At least I lived to tell the tale. So far."

He made it to the top and drew himself up to his full height and still he didn't feel tall enough, not in the eyes of this woman. He hated it. He really did. Because there was something incredibly special about her. She was easily balanced on her skis, leaning on her poles, serene and wholesome. She made his entire being, his entire spirit, take notice.

Suddenly, he was aware of someone else talking and then he remembered. There were two other women with Katherine. And as they were moving away, one was saying, "C'mon, Holly, let's go fetch that ski."

Ski. That didn't register either. There wasn't anything in this world but Katherine and the gentle quirk of her smile, and the thud of his pulse in his chest. She kept him glued in place. He could see her heart in her eyes. There wasn't a drop of judgment, nor was she silently teasing him even when he might deserve it.

"Jack, are you going to be able to make it down okay? Marin has her cell phone. She can call for the ski patrol."

"No!" He'd rather crash and burn and break every bone in his body—twice—than to admit defeat in front of Katherine. "I'm fine. It's already coming back to me. I think the fall knocked loose some forgotten knowledge inside my head."

"Good, because you could have been really hurt. I would hate to see that happen to you."

That comment was tough on a man's ego. Tough because she was concerned and caring. That made him like her even more.

"Guess I'll be going now. You want to catch up with your friends?"

She didn't budge. She didn't blink. The crinkle of a hint of a smile remained in the corners of her soft, pretty mouth. Snow flecked the fake-fur lining of her jacket collar and clung to the sleek matching ski cap. She looked like everything good and sweet in the world, and he didn't want to think this way about *this* woman.

"Uh, Jack? Before you take off you need to know something. You're missing a ski."

It registered vaguely. He straightened his shoulders, looking as tough and manly as possible, considering he only had one ski. "I'll take care of it."

"Are you sure?"

"Positive." He had to face it. He was never going to impress this woman—not that he even wanted to, of course. But *had* he wanted to, his dignity had passed the point of no return. He stabbed his poles into the hard berm of snow, ready to go. "Goodbye, Katherine."

Okay, she could take a hint. Katherine checked the trail for skiers, but no one was coming. She couldn't just leave him here—as Marin had put it, he was doom on two sticks—but she sensed his pride was bruised more than anything.

The poor man. He towered over her, a big

mountain of a guy, radiating capability and strength. He didn't look as though he had a single weakness. So why was it hard to find the will to kick off and leave him standing there?

She thought of what her friends and her sisters had said. She did not like this man, not like that, and she wasn't in denial about it. Really. So then, why did her heart crack just as little? And then a little more as she kicked off and away, swooshing over the iced, packed snow, leaving him behind? She could feel his gaze on her back like the press of the cold wind. As she negotiated the next curve, she glanced over her shoulder to see him standing there, looking as alone as she felt.

She spotted Marin and Holly waiting for her and she skidded to a rough-edged halt.

Marin was flushed with excitement. "When I talked to him on the phone, did I mention to you that I found out he isn't married? He's a widower."

Katherine couldn't stop the wave of sympathy for him. That was sad. It did explain the lack of a wedding ring.

"Did you see how he was looking at you?"

"Like I was contagious with the bird flu?"

"That's the denial talking." Holly held up

Jack's lost ski. "We would have returned this to him, but we didn't want to interrupt."

"There was nothing to interrupt." So maybe she was in a *little* denial. But not much. "I get the strong feeling that Jack doesn't like me at all."

"He does," Holly and Marin chimed in unison.

Did they know how wrong they were? Completely. "What do you two know about men? You're both single."

"Yeah, but we have the experience of many failed relationships between us. Here." Holly handed her the ski. "Either go up to him or we'll just wait around the next corner and you can wait here for him, since he's bound to come looking for this."

"Then he'll find it just fine, whether I'm here or not." She could see him starting down the trail, balancing on one ski. He was on his way down.

There was only one thing to do. She propped the slim black ski, brand-new and newly waxed, against the snow berm where it would be easy for Jack to spot when he limped around the corner. "You two have been plotting while I was talking to Jack."

"Guilty," Marin admitted. "He's a great-looking guy. He's a caring father, so I know he has a lot of heart."

"You can have him then, because his personality isn't so great." Katherine wasn't sure if that was the whole truth, but Jack's first impression had been a whopper. Remembering how he'd behaved when they'd first met would keep her firmly entrenched in her state of denial. "C'mon, let's get moving."

"You're just gonna leave the ski?" Holly looked crestfallen. "But, what about our plan? You can't get to know him better if you don't stay, talk, meet him in the lodge for hot drinks."

"News flash. I don't plan on seeing Jack Munroe ever again even if I have to avoid him. Let's go, he's almost here." She pushed off, leading the way down the trail. Snow pummeled into her like little wind-driven bullets, and she didn't look back. Didn't want to.

Because she already knew what she'd see. The disappointment on her friends' faces and Jack Munroe wobbling on one ski. Jack Munroe, who'd given her flowers and who had enough problems on his plate. Just because he was a widower didn't mean she was suddenly interested in him. She was pretty sure that Jack was not the man she was looking for.

* * *

Humiliation was a sad thing. Jack had found his ski, but his dignity had taken a fatal hit. In front of Katherine McKaslin.

Why her, Lord? He took another sip of strong sweetened tea in the warmth of the lodge's empty auxiliary dining room and tried to squeeze the memory from his mind of glancing up to see Katherine at the top of the ravine, looking like a gift from heaven dappled with snow.

The Lord wasn't answering, and Jack had to accept it. Why he was continuously coming across as a bull in a china shop in front of Katherine might forever remain a mystery. Maybe the trick would be staying away from her. That shouldn't be too hard to do, right?

Right. So stop thinking about her.

Okay, he focused on the view outside the wide picture windows. Stunning. The rugged snow-draped mountain peaks stabbed into the falling veil of snow. Closer in, the mountain slope lay in a pure mantle of white that felt as peaceful as it looked. Out front, just within his view, a half dozen teens on skis were clustered in a half circle around a beginning instructor. Hayden was one of them. She stood at the end, a little farther away than the others. He only saw her from behind but he knew that slump to her shoulders. She was scowling, looking nothing at all like the little girl he remembered.

Where had the time gone? In a blink of an eye, here she was, a teenager, fifteen going on sixteen, and he wasn't ready for it. Something had gone wrong somewhere, and he didn't know what. The move here to Montana, to a smaller city and a slower pace was supposed to fix that. And after the stunt she'd pulled in Katherine's store, it was clear his little girl was a teenager on the edge of trouble. Funny, he'd always blamed the parents for something like that.

But he was simply doing his best.

Maybe finding a church would help with that. He simply hadn't had the time with the move and the adjustment to a new home and job to start searching for the right one. Thank God for this opportunity. Jack's chest tightened with a mix of emotions he couldn't name except for one. Gratitude. If Hayden was going to act out, it had been a blessing that she'd done so in front of Katherine. That they'd been given this chance to make things right. It was an opportunity he refused to waste, and he wouldn't let Hayden waste it either.

Katherine. His guts knotted when he thought of her. Maybe the Lord was trying to tell him something. Like give up any thoughts of dating. You aren't cut out for it. Not that he'd been thinking on that real hard, but some of the guys at work were more than happy to offer to set him up. He'd turned them down, so far. He was doing fine enough on his own, right?

Well, as tough as it was to admit, not really.

"More tea, sir?" The sunny waitress breezed up to his corner table with another pot of steaming water.

Not in a sunny mood, he gave a gruff nod and kept his attention on Hayden. The snow was falling harder now, shadowing the kids so that it was hard to see them as they followed their instructor, sidestepping toward the beginner's run. He watched Hayden's blue parka grow smaller and disappear over a rise.

That's when he felt it, a flicker of emotion stretching tight right behind his sternum and then popping free, like a rubber band snapping. What was that?

He didn't have to look around to know who was coming his way. For some unfathomable reason, he could feel the string pulling tight again, right over his heart the moment he saw Katherine enter the dining room.

His gut instinct told him to duck, but it was too late.

Chapter Five

That man sitting at the window…there was something familiar about those mile-wide shoulders and the tidy shock of black hair. His posture was as rigid as a seasoned soldier's, and she'd seen that black parka before.

Jack Munroe. Her feet froze in place in the archway between the lodge's main restaurant and the practically empty room. Maybe he hadn't spotted her. It wasn't too late to tiptoe back out of the room.

Don't be silly, she told herself. She'd planned never to see Jack Munroe again. This was a co-incidence, not divine intervention or her secret wish. She'd simply find a quiet table on the far side of the dining room, pull out her book and wait for Holly and Marin to find her. She didn't have to look in Jack's direction whatsoever.

Luck might be in her favor. With the way he was gazing out the window, he might not even notice her. She could walk right past him. *If* he did happen to look her way, she'd toss him a polite smile. It sounded like a good plan.

So why did her feet take on a mind of their own and lead her to his table? "Did you ever find your lost ski?"

There wasn't an ounce of surprise on his chiseled face as he pivoted in his chair and fastened his gaze on hers. Total control emanated from him like cold from the window. "I did. After a few more runs, skiing came back to me."

"Good." Katherine hadn't spotted him on the advanced runs, so she guessed he'd tried a less challenging trail.

Well, she hadn't intended to chat and didn't want to. Time to make her escape. But the instant she took a step, his hand shot out and his fingers curled around her wrist. The shock of the contact startled them both.

"You can't go yet." He released her, but his gaze was pure black steel. "Not until I apologize."

She didn't know if it was fury at his overbearing manner or something like interest that froze her in place. The imprint of Jack's hand felt like a brand on her arm. "Apologize? For which offense?"

"Are there that many?"

"You know the answer to that."

"Sorry. I just—" Jack shook his head. What was he thinking? It had been a mistake to stop her. A mistake not to have kept as much distance between them as possible. "Is there any way we can start over?"

"Start over with what?"

She was going to make this as hard as possible. He squared his shoulders, ready to take a direct rejection. "We can pretend we didn't meet the way we did."

"You mean with your daughter stealing from my family's store and you trying to run over me with your car?" Her soft dainty mouth tightened into a thin line. One slim eyebrow shot up as if he'd insulted her.

She wasn't insulted, he realized. She was too nice a woman for that. He stood and pulled out the chair next to him. Watched deeper emotions play in her captivating eyes.

Whenever he was around her, he felt off-balance, as if he'd lost his center, his footing, everything he was sure of. Maybe she felt this, too. "If you can put those things behind you, I'd like to try again."

"What makes you think I want to?"

"Just a hunch. Cop's instinct."

"Let me guess. Your hunches are wrong a lot, aren't they?"

"You'll have to sit down and find out."

"Too bad I'm not the least bit curious." She smiled, and it was genuine. Her earlier veneer of politeness had vanished.

Did she have any idea of the effect she had on him? With her heart shining in her gentle eyes and shaping her sweet smile, he could see her brightness and goodness as clearly as the dimples in her cheeks.

It took all his effort to sound like a normal, unfazed guy just having a cup of tea. He tugged the chair beside him out a little more. "C'mon. Let's start over. I'm Jack Munroe."

"Are you always this bossy?"

"Mostly. It's what I do best."

That made her laugh. He liked the sound, quiet and sweet, just like her. "Being bossy isn't the best."

"It is when most of my traits are worse." He stood and held out his hand. "It's nice to meet you, Katherine. Sit down and have a cup of tea with me."

To his surprise, she placed her hand in his so they were palm to palm. But the casual contact didn't feel casual at all. Air shot out of his lungs and, overwhelmed, his every sense stilled.

Katherine didn't seem affected as she withdrew her slender hand and smoothly slipped into the empty chair. "I'm not sure this is a good idea."

"Sure it is." He commandeered a clean cup from the place setting on the neighboring table and poured. He'd have the waitress add it to his bill on her next pass through.

He pushed the steaming cup in her direction. She was just sitting there, looking elegant in a purple fuzzy sweater and wash-worn jeans. "Overconfidence is one of my other bad traits. Luckily I'm usually right. I get that you were up here to ski with your friends. Do you do that a lot?"

"At least once a week during the ski season. Why do you look so surprised?"

"Because you look like you belong on that figurine shelf in your store."

That was like a blow to her heart. Katherine reached for the sugar jar, noticed her hand was shaking and willed it to stop. "You think I'm cold. Remote. I've heard it before."

"Not even close. I meant that you look too elegant to know how to attack the advanced run like a pro." He paused to study her face. He must have caught some hint of the pain his comment had caused because he grimaced. "Now you know why I've never been able to remarry."

"Because you scare your dates away?"

"So fast that many have not waited until the meal was over to bolt."

That didn't surprise her either. "You do have a charming personality."

"Funny, I don't hear that often." He shrugged those big shoulders of his in an oh-well gesture. Apparently he'd been told this so often, it was hardly a blip on his radar screen.

At least he had a sense of humor, which was a redeeming quality. *Not* that she was noticing. She stirred sugar into her cup of tea. "I'm a little too tidy for most people. My sisters say I'm obsessive compulsive."

"You're just super-organized."

"True. Do you understand, because you're, uh, *super-organized,* too?"

"Guilty."

As she nudged the sugar jar in his direction, he reached before she let go and their fingers brushed. It was the slightest contact, but her heart stilled.

Okay, she was going to stay in denial about that, too.

"What happened to your friends?"

"Marin is leading the kids' prayer meeting. Holly is checking on her merchandise in the lodge's gift shop. She's a jewelry designer. So I thought I'd find someplace quiet and read while I wait for them."

"Read?"

"From my book." Which she pulled out of her bag. An Inspirational romance. "Marin mentioned that Hayden had joined the youth group ski program."

"I hope she's taking to skiing better than I did."

If she'd just met Jack, if the first time she'd ever met him was when she'd sat down at this table, she would have a much different opinion of him.

She also wouldn't have been able to give meaning to the shadows in his eyes, darker than his irises, more than skin-deep. Why was it that she could see into this man's heart? Behind the rugged man-in-charge demeanor was an honest guy, who wanted to do the right thing, who loved with all he had, who intended to fight for his daughter to get her in a good place.

"It's not my business," she cleared her throat, surprised at how thick and honest her voice sounded. Somehow he'd disarmed her controlled outer layer of defense. "Marin mentioned you were a single parent. It can't be easy for a dad to raise a teenage daughter."

"Not easy at all." Emotion flashed through his dark eyes and he turned away to stare out the long wall of windows where the veil of falling snow had thickened. "Heidi's been gone for three years."

"That had to have been devastating for both of you."

A single nod. He continued to stare out the window, stoic as chiseled granite. She felt the heavy weight of his sorrow. Was that why she felt an uncommon connection with Jack? They were two people who'd known loss and defeat? Maybe that's all this was, nothing romantic, nothing like destiny.

In a way, it was a relief to realize this. There was nothing to deny. Nothing to worry about. They were simply two people who'd walked a similar path in life. "I was ten when my mom left. She took our youngest sister and just walked out the door one day. It was summer, and she'd just pinned up the wash to dry on the backyard clothesline."

"Did she and your sister ever come back?"

Katherine stared out into the endlessly falling snow. "I can still see the load of T-shirts snapping in the breeze and smell the laundry-soap scent of them. Mom backed the family car out of the detached garage and took off down the alley. I saw glimpses of the car through the bowed heads of the sunflowers that lined the back corner of the fence, and then she was gone forever."

"That couldn't have been easy." Jack scrubbed a hand over his face. The burden of worry and responsibility he carried felt close to the surface. Maybe too close. "Your story gives me hope for my daughter. You went through losing your mom, too, and look how incredible you turned out. Hayden will, too."

"Wait one minute. I'm so far away from incredible that I can't believe you said that."

How perfect was Katherine? Not only was she wonderful but modest, too. "I'm not gonna argue with you about it. Learn to take a compliment."

"All right, but be sincere next time, instead of trying to be charming."

So, she thought he was charming? Talk about a good surprise. "Next time, huh? You mean there's a chance I might run into you somewhere sometime and you won't try to avoid me?"

"It does depend on how this turns out *and* how easy you are to avoid."

He took swig from his cup, and the tea tasted

better, sweeter. He couldn't say why. He had to admit that she'd made a dent in his defenses. Again. "How did you get past losing your mom?"

"I don't think I ever have."

He studied Katherine. She was still staring at the window, but she didn't seem to be seeing what was beyond the glass, or the thick snow falling ever harder.

"I think everyone has wounds in their lives. It's not so much that you erase that wound from your heart, as much as you learn to move past the pain. To live and learn to trust others even with that old wound." Katherine pivoted to assess him with those lovely unguarded eyes. It was easy to see beyond the calm controlled manner she showed the world to the real woman she kept private.

He liked *this* Katherine. "So, if you never got over it, will Hayden?"

"No."

Katherine's heart twisted tightly, protectively against the painful shards of the past brought to the surface. Also from Jack's wince of hope lost. He looked down at his capable hands, loosely fisted on the table, a strong towering man who looked defeated. She knew it wasn't the answer he had wanted to hear.

But it was the truth.

Why did she feel so much for him? She could tell herself she didn't like this guy, but it wouldn't be the truth. If she was one hundred percent honest, then she had to admit she did like him. There was no sense denying it. How could she not care for this man, the one beneath the mask of commander and protector? He radiated earnestness and integrity, and it touched her, for he had a heart to match.

Maybe she liked this Jack best of all.

"I'm out of my depth with Hayden, I'll admit to it. Just when I think I've got this parenting thing figured out, she goes and ups the ante on me."

"Plus, she's got you wrapped around her little finger."

"You're right about that." He shrugged, a gesture of defeat. "It's not a good thing, I know. I just can't help it."

"A teenager is an awesome responsibility. As much as you love your daughter, which is always a good thing, there's so much you can't protect her from. You would do anything to keep her safe."

He nodded once, staring out the window and not seeing anything at all. "Then what do I do? I can't accept the direction she's heading in. I won't let it happen. Somehow, I gotta get her through this. I'm at a loss. She was in counseling for a while and I thought she was doing better. Looking forward in her life, not back."

"That's a tall order for any of us. It takes a lot of time to get to those roots of pain. They can go deeper than you think."

"Speaking from experience?"

"It's the same road we're all on, right?" She tilted her head to the side, gazing up at him through her long, natural lashes. All honesty and compassion. "Life is a tough path to walk, and kids aren't immune to the struggles of it, no matter how a parent tries to shelter them."

"That's what I've worked hard for. To insulate her from anything that could hurt her. And when her mother died, there was no way to shield her from that. In trying to, maybe I got it all wrong. Maybe I've done more harm than good."

"I don't believe that for a minute."

As if her belief in him was the key to a lock within him, he felt a door give way and the truth tumble out. He was a man who prided himself on his strength and discipline. He was a do-the-right-thing kind of man, but as hard as he'd tried, with all the good intentions, still there were shattered pieces, like failure, tumbled, broken at his feet. "I've made mistakes."

"Who hasn't?" Her understanding made him feel less alone. Less confused. "After my mom left, Dad had such a hard time. We all did. Our world, as we knew it, had ended, and it was never the same again. But my dad, he held it together. He held us together."

"He sounds like a good man."

"That's my point, exactly. In the end, he is what mattered. Our mom may have left us, but our dad, he didn't. It took me a long time to get it, to understand that no matter how much it hurt when our mother left, it did not have the power of our dad's love and commitment to us. Some people you can count on no matter what. And that kind of love is more important and more powerful."

He felt too revealed. She'd gotten too close, and his instincts were bellowing at him to back up, close down, move as far away from this woman as humanly possible. He was riveted in place, torn. It wasn't only her understanding that had forged a connection between them. It wasn't that she'd said the right words at the right time or what he'd most needed to hear. He'd felt glimmers of this *before* she'd entered the lounge, before he'd barreled past her on the ski slope like a buffoon on two pieces of wood. Even before he'd brought the roses to her store.

You can't be interested in her because she's rejection waiting to happen. Women like her were a deep mystery to a straightforward, old-school man like him. Not that he had anything against career woman with fancy degrees—you only had to look at her to know she had one—but he had as much of a chance of understanding her as he did of taking a running leap and landing on the moon.

Maybe he'd been down the romance path too many times between his marriage and his previous dating attempts not to believe it was a path lined with thorns, not rose petals. Love was a dangerous proposition. If he asked her to dinner, she'd turn him down flat. Or would she?

"You seem like a good man, Jack. I know this will work out for Hayden. She's lucky to have a caring father in her corner. Just follow your heart. If you're listening, God will lead you in the right way."

"I know. Sometimes my reception gets a little static. Too much interference and it's hard to hear clearly." He took a sip of his tea, gone cool, and couldn't swallow past the emotion lumped in his throat. "Probably you don't know how that is."

"You would be wrong. The problem isn't

coming from above, but it's me. Always me. I don't know if I just can't let go of controlling my life, or if I just can't trust even God that much. I don't know."

Feelings came to life within his heart and weren't like anything he'd felt before. They were soft and warm, and as soothing as prayer. Tenderness lit him up from the inside out and he wanted… he didn't know what he wanted. But he liked being with her.

The storm of footsteps pounding behind him was his first clue. The shock of the air, like the stillness before a deadly lightning strike was the second. He was already turning in his chair when Hayden's fury hit.

"Daddy! What are you doing? Why are you with *her?*"

He rose to his full height, growing oddly calm as he stared down at his daughter. She was steaming mad, no mistake about that, not with the narrow, blazing eyes, pinched nostrils and the flat angry line of her mouth. She looked like Heidi in a full tantrum and it shook him to his soul. He opened his mouth to set her straight, but she was on a roll.

"Why are you with her? She ruined my life. This was all her stupid idea. You take me home. *Now.*"

A snorting bull would be calm next to the way he felt. "Enough." Over the sound of his voice echoing in the vast room, he turned to Hayden. "Apologize."

His pulse thundered in his veins as he took in Katherine's shocked and, to her credit, sympathetic look toward the teenager. He was aware of Hayden's rage and, underneath that, fear.

He wagered Katherine had just figured out the real reason he'd never been able to remarry.

Hayden hadn't been ready.

"It's okay, Jack." Katherine stood and collected her book and bag. Elegant, classy, as if she hadn't been touched by Hayden's insulting behavior. "Hayden, it's good seeing you again. I think I'll keep both of you on my prayer list."

She left, and it was like watching a dream walk away. Leaving him feeling empty, defeated, obliterating every bit of progress he'd made with Katherine. Obliterating any possibility, had there truly been one at all.

Chapter Six

By the time Katherine reached home, the snow had turned to a bitter rain. Marin and Holly had wanted to talk over what had happened, but she'd been running late and, besides, she wasn't up to it. That was the understatement of the century. What good came from rehashing the past? Not one thing.

What she needed was to retreat to her nice quiet condominium and dig some comfort foods out of the cupboards. Maybe, if she closed all the windows and locked the doors behind her she could escape the pieces of the past. Those broken pieces were razor-sharp.

Home. Finally. She pulled into her garage and hit the remote. The door slid down, shutting out her view of the world.

Good. Maybe she could shut out the

memories, too. Her stomach rumbled, but she couldn't feel her hunger. As she swung open the car door, the cold temperature didn't touch her, for she felt colder inside. Seeing Hayden tonight was like looking into her past. Looking at her biggest mistakes.

Katherine took a deep breath to try to clear away the feelings in her chest, feelings that did not seem to be her own, but they stuck like glue to the pieces of her past. They weren't going to be so easy to turn off and stuff back down. Maybe a vat of chocolate fudge ripple ice cream would help. At least it couldn't hurt.

It wasn't just the memories that were getting to her or the weight of the past. It was Jack, too. He'd gotten past her first walls of defense and she hadn't been able to shore up the breach.

She fumbled with her key ring in search of her deadbolt key, but the keys slipped through her fingers, crashed on the cement at her feet and went flying against the shadowed recycling bins.

Take a deep breath, Katherine, and think of the ice cream. If chocolate can't fix it, then prayer will.

Unexpectedly, the inside door whipped open and Ava stood in the brightness. With one look at her sister's sunny smile, some of the shadows in her heart receded. Katherine scooped up her keys and pocketed them. *Thank you, Father. My sisters are just what I need right now.*

"What are you doing?"

"I dropped my keys."

"Well come in. Danielle just got here with dinner. You don't look so good."

"I'm okay." She managed to stand, smoothing away her emotions. Behind Ava in the well-lit kitchen she could see her stepsister opening take-out cartons at the marble counter. Aubrey was helping her.

It was good to be home. The wonderful spicy tang of Chinese food drew her forward. The sight of Ava's signature fudge chocolate cream cookie crust pie was an answered prayer, the cheerful greetings from her sisters a precious blessing.

"Next week, maybe I'll tag along," Danielle said as she stuck a serving spoon in a huge carton of kung pao chicken. "If you don't mind and if the kids manage to stay healthy. I haven't hit the slopes since our big New Year's outing."

"You work too much." Aubrey grabbed a pile of plates from the cupboard over the dishwasher. "Besides, this is why you'll be eternally stuck on the bunny run. You don't practice."

"It *could* be that I'm not athletic in the slightest." Danielle swished a lock of dark hair behind her ear, smiling easily, but the slight strain always showed whenever she was around them. It always had. Blended families weren't as simple as prime time sitcoms made them out to be. Danielle sighed, and the strain smoothed from her heart-shaped face. "Katherine, you look exhausted. Sit down. I've got a pot of tea steeping on the table."

"Thanks, Dani." Katherine shrugged out of her coat. She'd managed to leave everything in the car, including her purse. "But no waiting on me, okay? You work hard enough keeping up with your little ones."

"I do work hard." On her way to the fridge, Danielle shouldered past Ava who was counting forks out of the drawer. "Unlike the twins."

"Hey, why do you say it like that? I work. A little."

"At least I have a job," Aubrey argued from the counter. "So, Kath, are you gonna tell us the scoop? Or do we have to torture it out of you?"

"The scoop?" Thank heavens that her sisters had no idea she'd had a run-in with Jack on the mountain. And a sort of, well, bonding experience. Whatever she wanted to call it, her time with him had been illuminating, hopeful and disastrous all at the same time.

It took talent to turn a pleasant cup of tea and conversation with an available man into a totally devastating experience. Which she wasn't about to share with anyone, even her sisters, whom she loved most in the world. It was best to sound indifferent; maybe the fervor over those white roses would blow over faster.

She took a plate from the top of the stack on the edge of the island and started the serving line. The twins were arguing about their jobs and their lack of full-time work outside the family business, and Danielle was stressing over the sweet and sour sauce she'd forgotten to pour over the pork. "We're missing Rebecca. She couldn't make it?"

"She had some kind of lab thing for one of her classes." Ava grabbed a plate and dug into the carton of moo gao gai pan. Chunks of chicken and vegetables tumbled onto her plate and the counter. "Oops. Back to the scoop. Has Jack called you yet?"

"No. And I'm absolutely positive that he won't."

Wasn't that the truth? She remembered the look on Jack's face when his daughter had started yelling. It wasn't likely she'd forget Hayden's words or how it felt to see a teenager almost the age... Don't think about that, Katherine.

Danielle looked scandalized. "How could this guy not like you? He's the one who brought the roses, right?"

"As a thank-you, not as a romantic thing." Katherine moved on to the noodle chow mein and, in need of comforting carbs, piled it high. Thank heavens there was pork-fried rice, too. "Let me repeat that, since the twins are hard of hearing. It's not a romantic thing. It's just impossible, end of story."

"Hey, we're not hard of hearing—" Ava protested.

"—It's just that we know something you don't," Aubrey finished.

"I'm not even going to ask." Katherine looked to Danielle. "How are the kids?"

"I signed Tyler up for swimming lessons." Danielle, the perfect housewife and mom, calmly redirected the conversation, bless her. "They have baby swimming lessons, too, so I broke down and put Madison in a class, although I have to go in with her, and I'm *not* a swimmer. Luckily we stay in the shallow end. We'll see how it goes."

"You'll do fine." Katherine looked down at her full plate. No more room, so she got out of Ava's way and met her stepsister's gaze. There was a greater sadness there, the kind a woman rarely spoke of. Or even examined for herself in quiet times. "If you don't like it, let me know. I'll go in the water with her, and you can watch safe and dry from the benches."

"Thanks." Dani reached out and laid her hand on Katherine's. The slight squeeze said more than thanks, more than understanding. It went deeper. "If this guy, the one who brought the roses, isn't the kind of man to accept what happened to you, then he isn't good enough for you. Don't forget that."

What did you do when you feared the kind words of your family were only that? Kind words. The truth was that people could be tough and cold at heart, and she'd already lost the chance for marriage once because Kevin had refused to understand.

She squeezed Dani's hand right back, her sister not of blood but of circumstance. The Lord in His benevolent wisdom was ever gracious. "C'mon, sit by me. We got in these great new picture books at the store this morning. I haven't even shelved them yet, but they are just adorable. I brought a copy home for Madison."

Ava and Aubrey were waiting at the dining-room table, plates piled high, tea poured and steaming. "Hurry up," they said in unison. "We're starving."

Katherine took her seat and bowed her head for the blessing, grateful for her sisters. She was glad not to be alone with visions of her past or thoughts of Jack Munroe.

Home. It ought to be a man's castle, a place where he could leave his troubles at the door. Home hadn't been that for Jack in a long while. For so long, peace was only a memory gone dim with time. Tonight, there would be no peace, he knew. One look at his daughter's face told him that. As she burst through the garage door and tore through the kitchen toward the stairs and her room, he knew that she thought she had the upper hand.

Maybe the truth was that she did and had for a long time. He was only seeing it now. In his attempts to make her happy, to keep her calm, to appease his guilt, he'd been reacting to her behavior instead of directing it.

"Sit down, young lady." He let the door bang closed for effect. "At the table."

"I'm going to my room. I'm upset."

"Not as upset as you've made me." When she kept going he raised his voice. "You have one extra week of volunteer work. I'll be happy to make it more."

She hesitated. He saw her weighing her

options. Then she gave a strand of blond hair a flip behind her shoulder and took the stairs.

"Did I mention that volunteer work will be in Katherine McKaslin's book store?"

That got her attention. She whirled around, horrified. "Daddy, no! I *hate* that lady."

"Katherine McKaslin is the reason you aren't facing shoplifting charges."

"She can afford it. Jan says that her family has all kinds of money—" She stopped, eyes widening from anger to horror as she realized what had slipped out.

"You are still seeing Jan even though I forbade you to."

"We go to the same school. We have like tons of classes together. I *can't* avoid her. It'd be *rude*."

"You have no problem being rude to Miss McKaslin. You disobeyed me, Hayden. Again."

"Sorry, Dad. It's like the only time." She turned on the Bambi eyes, the innocent sweet look that he'd bought every time. Because he'd wanted to. Because he could not believe that his little girl was anything but good and innocent and sweet. But the years following Heidi's death had been troubled ones at best. There had been problems at work, and problems at home. Grief, his and Hayden's. Anger, his and Hayden's. He'd had long workdays and endless overtime.

Maybe, after what he'd learned about Heidi, he'd needed to believe there was innocence somewhere. So he'd never even noticed the small things until they were too big to ignore. Until now.

"The week of volunteer work is for the lie." He kept talking over his daughter's blowup. The trick was to be louder and stay that way. Eventually, what he was saying would sink in. "I'm taking you out of public school and enrolling you in another one. I'm sure Pastor Marin has a good suggestion for a private Christian school in the area. Uniforms will probably be mandatory, so that should solve your problem with inappropriate choices when it comes to your school wardrobe."

Since she was grounded until eternity anyway, he figured he had things pretty well under control. And wasn't that the key? "Now up to your room. I want you to think about what you've done. And how you're going to apologize to Miss McKaslin."

He waited, watching as his little girl gnashed her teeth and clenched her fists. "I'd be more than happy to make it another week."

Hayden kept whatever she wanted to say to herself, pivoted on the landing and stormed the rest of the way up the stairs and slammed her bedroom door. The entire house vibrated from the shockwave.

He got out a pound of hamburger and a skillet. While the hamburger was browning, he pawed through the pantry. His mind kept going back not to his little girl's behavior but to the look on Katherine's face. Of sadness. Of regret. Of understanding. Something she'd said bugged him and he kept coming back to it.

…everyone has wounds in their lives. It's not so much that you erase that wound from your heart, as much as you learn to move past the pain. He wondered what else had happened in her life to make her so wise when it came to deep wounds of the heart.

Then again, she was right. Life was a tough path to walk. No one was immune from that, no matter how it looked from the outside. Miss Katherine McKaslin looked like she had it going on; she was smart, kind, savvy and warm. She was faithful and principled and a fine example of what a woman should be.

A fine woman who made his heart beat inside out. A personable, gentle lady who'd laughed at his wry sense of humor and made him feel like the kind of man he wanted to be. A man unjaded by life and able to believe real love was out there. Not elusive like a rainbow's end, but within his reach.

Man, you keep thinking like that, and you're doomed to disappointment. The hamburger was sizzling, and he stirred it around in the skillet. He owed Katherine an apology, but he couldn't start thinking there could be more to it than that. He had Hayden. He had a full plate of problems. He'd be smart to stop glancing at the phone and stop wondering if Katherine was listed in the white pages, and get the green beans in a saucepan. He had to fix dinner, not start a romance.

He didn't have a chance with Katherine McKaslin. He had to face the truth. She wasn't interested in him. She probably wasn't sitting at home this exact minute wishing they'd had more time to talk, or wishing she'd gotten to know him better.

Nope, he was a realist. He stirred in a package of seasoning and noodles, covered the pan and left it to simmer, and went back to the pantry. It wasn't a matter of should he call Katherine, no, that had no place in his life. Or did it?

He'd think on that later. Right now, deciding between green beans or corn for dinner, and how to deal with Hayden when she came down to eat was enough to handle.

* * *

It's not any of my business, Katherine reminded herself as her gaze strayed to the kitchen phone. As she divided up the leftover Chinese food between her and Danielle, she tried not to wonder how Jack and Hayden were doing. The twins had already left to catch a movie at the discount theater near the college. Danielle was busily wiping off countertops with a sponge, efficient and hard-working as always.

Katherine didn't know what she would have done without her stepsister.

"There. It's almost as spotless as before we came." Dani rinsed the sponge at the sink. "The twins upset you, didn't they? You wouldn't show it, but I can tell."

"They get this way about every man *they* think is a possibility for me. A few weeks ago it was the copier repairman. That's why the store's copy machine is on the fritz and I won't get it fixed. I'm not bringing that man into the store again and get Ava going on this *path*." Katherine sighed, exhaling pent-up frustration she didn't know she had. She fetched a plastic grocery bag from the bin under the kitchen sink, neatly piled Danielle's share of the food into it and gave it a shove in Dani's direction.

"Katherine? You seem off tonight. Is it something to do with this new guy the twins mentioned? Do you need to talk?"

Katherine shook her head. She needed to talk, but she didn't know if she was ready. "I thought you wanted to get home for Madison's bedtime."

"I always have time for you. Always have, always will."

No one knew the way Dani did how hard times had been for her and the hard choices she'd had to make. "Go home to your little ones. Hug them tight and keep them safe."

"I guess that's answer enough. For now." Dani took the bag and her car keys. "But I'm going to stop by the store tomorrow morning. In case you're ready to talk then. We could go out for coffee. Spence can run the store alone for a few hours."

"It's a deal." Katherine knew she wouldn't want to talk then. There were some things she never wanted to think about, ever, much less talk about as casually as the weather. But she appreciated Danielle's support. "You've got the new book?"

"Right here." Dani stopped to put on her coat. "Maybe this new man, this white-roses guy, he could be the one who—"

"I just don't think so. I want to get close to a good man, but trusting him? That's the problem. Love is very dangerous."

"It's like getting onto a sinking ship. But sometimes, together, you can get it to sail." Why Dani looked sad when she said that, Katherine didn't know. "If you have his number, you should call him. Invite him to church."

"Do *you* need to talk?"

"You're changing the subject." Dani gave her a hug. "It was one mistake in judgment long ago. The consequences were devastating. I was there, I know. But you deserve to be happy. Not every man is Kevin. Not every man is going to judge and sentence you for what another man did against your will."

"I know." She knew that. Logically, she knew. But her heart? Her spirit? They were more tentative. "My problem is finding a good man. A truly good man. Since I'm not interested in the copier repair guy."

"You need to start dating again."

"Dating. Ugh." Anxiety pooled in her stomach. "After every date I've been on in the last year—not that it's been that many—I get home and vow, never again. I hate dating."

"How are you going to find the right man with that attitude?"

"I know, but I have to face the facts. All the good ones are already married. Those men get snatched up early. And now that I'm over thirty, I'm looking at what's left over. Believe me, you don't want to date left-overs. There's always something really wrong with them, which is why they haven't married in the first place, or some perfectly nice woman married them, brought them home, got to know them and then threw them back in the dating pond."

"Excuses, excuses." Danielle's smile was gentle. "Jonas has known this guy since they were kids. He's new to the area. He's a good, solid faithful man. We could fix you two up."

"I'd rather get a root canal without anesthetic. I've given up on dating."

"Never give up, Katherine. God will send the right man to you. I believe that with all my heart."

"Go home to your babies. Give them extra snuggles from their Aunt Katherine."

"Okay, but we'll talk about this tomorrow at the coffee shop. Good night."

"'Night." She threw the deadbolt, watching Danielle trudge down the dark, slick walkway to the sidewalk and then on to the guest parking.

Katherine changed rooms, standing in the bay front windows in the living room to keep

Dani in her sight and make sure she got to her car all right.

Never give up, Katherine. God will send the right man to you. Dani's words replayed in her mind as she watched the minivan back out of a parking spot and zip down the driveway, out of sight.

Katherine closed the blinds. She wanted Danielle to be right. That Mr. Right, not Mr. Almost-Right, was out there somewhere. Why did she hope, down deep, that man was Jack?

Because you like him more than you want to admit, Katherine, that's why. What she needed to do was to give it to the Lord and trust Him to handle it. Maybe the angels could send her a sign, too, so she would know when the absolute right man came along. A great big sign, one she couldn't miss.

Chapter Seven

"I don't believe it." Katherine had to look twice to make sure that she wasn't imagining Jack Munroe getting out of a black SUV in the small coffee shop's parking lot. She had a clear view of him, since she was sitting right in front of the window. "What are the chances?"

"Of what?" Dani peered over the rim of her cup and followed Katherine's gaze. "Who's that? Oh, is it the white roses guy? That's Jack Munroe?"

"Good guess."

"Before you got home last night, the twins described him in good detail. He *is* impressive."

"It's the scowl. It put me off at first, too. I think he comes across gruff on purpose." Katherine wrenched her gaze from him and twisted in her seat. She was in plain view, if he came up to the door. With any luck, he was going to the sandwich shop next door. If he did, then he could miss her entirely.

Lord, please let him be going to the sandwich shop.

Katherine propped her elbow on the table and hid the side of her face with her hand. He'd breached the outer layer of her defenses last night and she still felt vulnerable. Dangerously vulnerable. She didn't want to get close to a man who could see right into her. What if he saw too much?

She had to admit she liked him. She really did. What scared her more was the possibility that he might like her back. But all she had to do was remember Hayden's tantrum in the ski lodge to know the chances of it working out between her and Jack were slim to none. She didn't have to be a NASA scientist to know that.

Jack hesitated on the sidewalk between the two shops. Rainwater dripped off his baseball hat brim as he stood talking with someone just out of sight.

Dani leaned far forward over the table and craned her neck to get another good look at Jack. "Wow, he's all man, isn't he? He just radiates power. He looks intimidating, but I bet he's a teddy bear at heart. He has nice eyes, warm and kind."

"Stop looking at him, Dani. The last thing I want to do is—" to feel as I did when I was with him. She ached with a powerful regret she couldn't explain. It made no sense, but she knew it was best to avert her gaze, lean just right so he was less likely to see her.

I'm not being rude or cowardly, really.

Father, please, let him go on by. She held her breath, peeling off a layer from her chocolate croissant on the plate in front of her, waiting, willing Jack to go into the sandwich shop. To her surprise, he strode powerfully out of her range of sight. She waited a beat, but he didn't come back.

Thank you, Lord. Relief left her dizzy.

"It's for the best," she said, but she didn't know if she was trying to convince her stepsister of that. Or herself.

"So," Dani began. "About the guy Jonas knows. We could have you both over to dinner at our house. Or, we could meet you at a restaurant. Or you could just be brave and do the whole blind-date thing. Let him come pick you up, take you out, bring you home. Think of all that time you could talk and get to know him. It *could* be good."

"It could be doom."

"It could be *good.* C'mon, say yes."

"How about I think about it?"

"Deal. Think about it before you say yes. I won't take no for an answer." Danielle smiled as she cut into her chocolate chip muffin.

A blind date? Not in this lifetime. She wasn't about to change her mind, either. Katherine's gaze drifted to the empty sidewalk where Jack had been standing.

Well, one thing could change her mind, a small voice within her said. But she decided not to listen to it. After all, a girl had to be sensible.

In the sandwich shop, Jack stared at the menu. His eyes wouldn't focus. He wanted coffee. Just coffee. Maybe a muffin or something sweet. But when he'd spotted Katherine McKaslin in the coffee shop, looking as pretty as spring in a pink fuzzy sweater and tan slacks, he couldn't face her. Mostly because she hadn't acted the least bit interested in him. And after Hayden's outburst, he knew she never would be.

Let it go, man. He swiped his hand over his face, feeling exhausted and every minute of his thirty-six years. He'd hardly slept a wink last night, and it was one of his nights off, too, and so that meant he was starting work tonight already behind.

Pastor Marin had answered her office phone at exactly five minutes after eight and was more than happy to recommend a private Christian school that just happened to have a mandatory dress code. He'd spent the first part of the morning battling Hayden and getting her enrolled.

That had been enough to deal with. He didn't have the energy to try to face Katherine and apologize. He had the sinking feeling that there were no words in the English language sincere enough to ask for understanding for Hayden's outburst.

"Sir?" the college-age girl asked from behind the glass case. "What can I get you?"

"Coffee," he managed to get out. "You got anything for a late breakfast?"

"I have some ham and egg breakfast sandwiches left."

It would do. He nodded, pulling out his wallet. What he didn't like was that Jonas, who was currently studying the chalkboard menu, was no dim bulb. He was going to figure out what was bugging him. A man could only get this knotted up over a woman. He'd better pull it together, fast.

Jonas ordered, and they took their trays to one of the scarred wooden tables. Was it coincidence or providence that he had a clear view of the sidewalk in front of the coffee shop?

Don't think about Katherine, he told himself, as he bowed his head for prayer.

Jonas said the blessing and then dug into his mid-morning ham on rye. "Now that you've got your girl settled, I've got someone I want to set you up with. My wife suggested it."

"A blind date? Forget it." He emptied three sugar packets into his coffee. "The last one I had was a full-out disaster. I vowed never again."

"And how long ago was this?"

"About a year. Around the time I started thinking about relocating to Montana." Jack would always be grateful to his childhood friend for helping him to get on with the state force, but friendship and gratitude only went so far. "No offense, but forget it. No. Won't do it. Not even at gunpoint."

"How are you supposed to find a nice lady to marry with that attitude?"

Good question. It wasn't just his attitude, but that of his fifteen-year-old daughter, too. And that was an even bigger obstacle. "I've got enough on my plate."

"Would it make a difference if I told you my wife is next door with her, right now? We were going to try to get you in the same spot, but you refused to go to the coffee shop."

Katherine was in that coffee shop. Jack gulped down a few swallows of coffee. What were the chances? "Who is she, the woman you were going to fix me up with?"

"My wife's stepsister. She's the nicest, most honest woman in the whole state of Montana. Her name's Katherine."

Jack choked, and that's when he saw her. Katherine McKaslin looking amazing in a sleek fashionable tan jacket, which she was buttoning as she paused on the sidewalk, beneath the awning, chatting with another woman—Jonas's wife. They were close, he guessed, by the way they leaned toward one another, relaxed and casual, but there was an obvious respect and a fondness between them. Like blood sisters have.

In that moment, time slowed to a stop. This was the Katherine from last night, honest and unguarded, all heart. A longing he couldn't name rushed through him, so sweetly his spirit ached. He watched as she waved goodbye to her friend, stepped off the curb in her low-heeled tan shoes and hurried through the parking lot, taking his heart with her.

A definite sign.

Funny how falling for someone could really sneak up on a guy. He took another swallow of coffee, but it had no taste. He watched Katherine weave through the second and third row of cars and then disappear, leaving only cold gray rain in his world.

The bookstore's mid-afternoon lull was in full swing, and Katherine was thankful. Ever since she'd returned from coffee with Dani, there had been constant customers. Not really a rush, but with the skeleton staff for the slow retail months following the new year, it kept everyone hopping.

Rain tapped cozily at the window of her office while she turned to her engagement book, which was open on her desk blotter. Several items on her to-do list had been crossed off, but there was still a long list needing to be done. The most important being, to figure out how to fix the copier. Or look up a different repair company in the phone book. Spence wasn't going to like that, so she continued down her list.

Prepare the journal entries for the bookkeeper. Katherine skipped right over that one, too. Usually she liked to get things done, but she was low on energy—on everything—today. She was not in the mood to deal with numbers or math.

There was a light knock on her open door. She turned to see Kelly standing just outside the door frame. "There's some people to see you."

"Customers?" At least she hoped it wasn't the copier repair guy. Spence could have made the call on his own initiative and forgotten to tell her.

"Not exactly." She lowered her voice, her expression cheerful. "It's that handsome cop guy. You know, with the shoplifter daughter."

I'd rather deal with the copier man. Katherine pressed her hand to her forehead. A headache was building there. "What do they want?"

"He wouldn't say. He just asked to see you. I think it's personal. Remember what you always tell me? Good things happen to good people."

She hopped out of her chair before Kelly could start. She tended to side with Ava and Aubrey on the subject of Jack Munroe. "I'll deal with him. Thanks."

"Sure. I'll be here, at the front, if you need anything."

Katherine ignored the knowing grin Kelly flashed her because she felt an icy tingling settle into the back of her neck, like doom.

Sure enough, there was Jack at the counter, his daughter at his side. Katherine took a step toward them and the icy tingle of nerves slid down her spine and into her stomach, from dread or attraction, she didn't know which. Probably a little of both.

"Katherine." He boomed her name. "Just the lady I'm looking for."

Hopefully, he didn't mean that literally. He was wearing civilian clothes instead of his trooper's uniform, but even in a sweatshirt and jeans, he looked mighty. There didn't seem to be a soft spot or a weakness in a man like that. If she didn't know he was a pretty nice guy, she never would have guessed it.

She swallowed hard, hoping her anxiety would settle, and approached the counter. With a little effort, she was able to smile cordially up at him, as if there was nothing between them. "What can I do for you two?"

"May I talk with you in private?"

Private. The butterflies in her stomach fluttered harder. "Sure. Come into my office. Kelly, would you mind being in charge until I get back?"

"No prob." Kelly, who often studied in the lull between customers, closed her college sociology book with a thud. She apparently was going to keep a sharp eye on Hayden.

Not that Katherine was worried about it. She thought the teenager looked different today, in a prep school uniform and blond hair without blue highlights. She looked almost contrite. "Hayden, there's hot herbal tea and cookies on the cart in the reading area, if you want to snack."

Hayden stared hard at the front door, as if hoping for a quick escape. "Whatever."

"All right. Jack, come on back." Katherine took a steadying breath and led the way into her office. The adequately sized room seemed to shrink as he entered, dominating everything in her sight.

She pushed the door almost closed, leaving an inch or so, and returned to her chair behind the desk. He'd crossed to the overstuffed chair into which he folded his imposing frame, dominating that, too.

He was a big man but the truth was, he'd become larger in her eyes. Better. She could no longer look at him and see only the tough, exacting officer of the law. She saw the real Jack, too. "I hope you didn't come to apologize about last night."

"Partly."

"It's not necessary."

"It is. Hayden behaved horribly. I can't apologize for her, she'll have to do that herself, but I should have made her do it on the spot. I was just so angry and disappointed in her, I didn't think of it."

"I was more concerned about how she's really doing. I get the feeling she's very insecure when it comes to you."

"You got the feeling, huh? Her shouting wasn't a definite clue?" Jack smiled. He liked that Katherine was so kind to his daughter— and she had reason not to be. "I suppose it's a logical thing. You lose one parent, you worry about losing the other one."

"Exactly. She's the reason you haven't re-married."

"The biggest reason. Other than the fact that women meet me and run for their lives."

"You exaggerate."

"I do. It's easier to do that, to make a joke of it than to admit the truth." Even that was too much, so he changed the subject. "I'm here because I liked your idea of volunteer work for Hayden. She's already worked one Saturday at the soup kitchen. I'm good with that, but I think Hayden needs to do more. She caused harm here and she needs to make amends to you."

"That's not necessary, Jack."

"I think it is, so I'm asking you to do me this

favor. Let her volunteer here. She comes with an attitude, and I'm sorry for that."

"I'm not afraid. Besides, attitudes have a way of adjusting themselves given a little time."

"Then you'll do it?" He leaned forward in the chair, his dark gaze locking on hers.

She felt the impact in her heart and she was falling. Just falling. "I'm not looking for free help, although I'd be happy to do whatever good I can for you."

"Is that what you do with your life, all the good you can?" He stood, towering over her desk, and made the nerves in her stomach worse.

She couldn't answer. Oxygen caught in her throat and refused to move. She felt her heart lurch, like a bird taking flight, and how silly was that?

"My Hayden is yours weekdays, except for youth group activities. You still have my home number?"

Somehow, she managed to nod.

"Then if she gives you any trouble—any at all—tell me and I'll take care of it. You deserve good things, Katherine. You're quite a lady."

Her jaw dropped. Every neuron in her brain misfired. She sat paralyzed in her chair as he left, closing the door behind him with a click.

She didn't know what to think.

* * *

You're quite a lady. Hours later, on his late-night dinner break, Jack still couldn't believe he'd said that. There's nothing like tipping your hand, buddy, and he'd probably made a big fool of himself. Wait, there was no probably about it. He knew he'd been a complete buffoon because she'd sat there in shock. Probably in horror. Speechless at hearing how he thought she was *quite a lady.*

Smooth, Jack. Real smooth. It was no wonder he was destined to be unmarried for the rest of his natural life. God was probably taking pity on nice women like Katherine and doing everything He could to keep them safe from non-suave men like him. Lord knows he hadn't been the best husband. He'd let his wife down.

"More hot water?" The waitress stopped with a hot water carafe and refilled the teapot on his table. "Would you like anything else? We've got a real nice apple pie tonight."

"Sure. Why not?" He unwrapped another tea bag and dunked it into the pot to steep.

Somehow he had to get his mind off Katherine. It wasn't going to be easy. So he flipped open his phone and dialed home, just to check on Hayden before her bedtime. But when Mrs. Garcia answered, she said that Hayden had gone to bed early. Maybe that was a good sign, he reasoned as he pocketed his phone. She'd put in a long day between the new school and working at the bookstore, and she'd been tired.

Thank God. He bowed his head and asked the Lord to help guide him, to keep leading him in the right direction. He prayed these changes for Hayden were the right ones.

When he unfolded his hands, the waitress was coming his way with a big triangle of pie. He couldn't say why he felt so alone as he grabbed a fork and dug in. Truth was, he couldn't remember feeling lonelier. It was a down-deep, all-encompassing lonesomeness. You'd think he'd be used to it by now.

But he didn't like it. Not one bit.

When he thought of Katherine, it just got worse. What was he gonna do about that?

In the loneliness of her dining room, Katherine turned the page in her gardening book and stabbed another chunk of warmed-up Chinese food with her fork. The noodle chow mein was tricky and the second she opened her mouth, the food tumbled off the fork and onto her napkin.

This is what she got from reading and eating at the same time. She crumpled the food-splotched napkin and tossed it onto the table, reached for a fresh napkin from the holder she kept handy and went back to her reading. Wiser this time, she skipped the noodles and stabbed a chunk of chicken. When she lifted that to her mouth, it fell off, too.

She had the irrational urge to blame Jack Munroe for it. She'd been off ever since he'd made that comment in her office. Now she couldn't stop wondering. Did Jack like her?

No, of course he didn't. Whatever was going on was a one-sided thing, right? She sort of, kind of, *maybe,* just a little, was starting to like him.

Okay, it wasn't just a little, it was a lot. Not that anything would come of it, of course.

She went back to her book but the words didn't make sense. It might as well be written in Greek for all she was understanding about how to grow new rose plants from cuttings. Forget it. She snapped the book shut. She'd worry about that later.

As for Jack, she'd do best to get her feelings for him under control. She liked him, but that's all there was to it. She had to be sensible. If he was interested in her, he would have let her know by now.

Besides, it had to be impossible. His beloved daughter hated her. She hardly knew anything about Jack, not really, not enough to predict how he would be as a boyfriend and, if it came to that, a husband. After all, a girl had to be sensible and think ahead.

And looking ahead, all she saw were big question marks. Huge question marks. Especially the biggest one of all. If Jack knew why Kevin had called off their wedding, would Jack agree with him? Or would he understand?

She didn't know him well enough to know either way.

Stop thinking about him, Katherine. You've given it up to God, remember? Let it go.

The phone rang. She snagged the extension in the kitchen. The caller screen said it was Jack Munroe. She stared at his name, not completely comprehending at first.

It was Jack. Her heart seized and stopped beating entirely. So, what should she do? Did she pick it up or let it ring?

Chapter Eight

"Katherine? It's Jack." After so many rings, he was taken by surprise when she answered. He took a deep breath. Brace yourself for her to hang up on you, man. "Jack Munroe."

But she didn't hang up. Her voice sounded strained. "Hi. What can I do for you?"

Was there a reason she was using her bookstore voice? Jack felt his courage begin to deflate a little. She was probably wondering how he had gotten her number. "I called your store and wound up talking to your brother. He was working late and suggested I give you a call."

"You were wondering how it went with Hayden today?"

"Right." That was one reason for calling, anyway. He stirred sugar into his teacup, the noises of the diner fading into silence. The only thing he could hear was the atomic-bomb caliber of his pulse booming in his ears. He couldn't remember being this nervous. Ever. "How did she do?"

"Okay, I guess. I assigned her to Ava, to help inventory the shipments that had come in and were piling up. I thought it was best if she didn't work directly underneath me at first, anyway. She doesn't seem to like me."

"I'm sorry about that." Jack winced. Hayden not liking Katherine would be a huge impediment if they were to start dating. *If* Katherine might be amenable to going on a date with him. This was the mission behind his call. "I wanted to make sure she behaved herself."

"I can honestly say she didn't hide the fact that she wasn't thrilled to be there, but she did fine. I was locked in my office with my brother going over the month-end expenses, so I hardly poked my head out of the door. But Ava had no complaints and, believe me, if she'd had any, I would have heard them. *You* would have heard them."

"That's a relief." That was the understatement of the century. He felt as if a lot was riding on this; that proved how much he liked Katherine—and hadn't yet admitted it to himself.

Although his *you're quite a lady* comment ought to have been a blazing clue. "You sure she didn't stage a coup d'état? I told her to be respectful."

"No military takeovers, but there's always tomorrow."

He could feel Katherine's smile across the line. He liked that. "It's too early to say, but one day down without doom is a good sign."

"Any step in a positive direction is a good one." Katherine cringed. Had she really said something so lame? Yes. Probably, if she could get past being nervous, she could think of something more interesting to say. Too bad she couldn't think of anything. Too bad she was trembling. She took a deep breath, hoping Jack would say something and rescue her. Silence stretched across the line. Say something, Jack.

He did. "So, how are things going with you?"

"Fine."

More silence stretched painfully between them. She could picture Jack on the other end grimacing, *so* wishing he hadn't called her.

See, this is where being a cool, in-control, confident woman of the world would come in handy. Too bad she was just sensible Katherine. *This* is why dating was so painful. She was definitely saying no to Danielle's blind-date guy. "Things are fine, other than my brother is stressing over the budget. My sisters are over-involved in my life and are trying to find me men to marry, but that's nothing unusual."

Why did she say that? That was way too personal. Now she was just talking out of sheer nervousness. Why was it getting worse? Her knees weakened and she had to sit down. The only consolation she had was Jack would probably hang up and be glad.

Instead, he chuckled. "Who are they trying to marry you off to?"

"A few weeks ago it was the copier repair-man. Who, I suspect, sabotaged the copier he was doing maintenance on after Ava hinted that I would be at the church's over-thirties singles night and maybe he should come, too."

"Wait a minute. You think he broke the copier on purpose, so he'd have a reason to come back and see you?"

"Considering he'd just packed his toolbox out the door when I went to make a bunch of copies and the machine sat there as dead as a doorknob. He'd conveniently left his business card on the table with a note on the back that said, 'no service charge for your next call.' Ava took it as a sign."

"Do you like this copier guy?"

"I've skipped the last two singles meetings at church just in case he's there."

"When's the next meeting?"

"Tomorrow night at seven. Marin hosts it, and I'm afraid she's going to highjack me and drag me to the next one. I can only hope the repair guy isn't there."

"And the copier?"

"Still broken. Until Spence notices, and then he's going to call to get it repaired. I'm praying, and I'm making my sisters pray, too, that he doesn't notice. You're laughing."

"Guilty." Jack chugged down the last swallows of tea. The noise of the restaurant and the hustle and bustle around him remained in the distant background next to Katherine's voice, her...*everything*.

"You think I'm a coward, don't you? I know, there are days I wish I had more bravado."

"You're just too nice to let anyone down. Or to say no if it would hurt their feelings. Right? So, what about the other guy?"

"What other guy?"

"The one your sisters are trying to fix you up with now?"

Okay, now her hands were starting to shake, too. An even worse situation. Jack was just making friendly conversation, right? He was probably on his dinner break, alone, wanting someone to talk to. Then why was he talking about *this?* "Oh, just some guy."

"Are you going to avoid him like the copier repairman? Or are you looking for a lawyer or an orthodontist or a heart surgeon?"

Where had he gotten that idea? "The job isn't as important as the man. I'm looking for someone good, faithful and sincere with a sense of humor, a big heart and the right values."

"Where do you stand on kids?"

"I like them. Either preexisting or in the future." Why the questions? "How about you? You said you haven't dated in a while."

"And I think you know why. Whatever I do, it's gotta be best for Hayden." Jack paused and silence settled into the line again, tense between them. "I'd like to start dating. Maybe there's a woman out there somewhere who wouldn't run from me during the course of a meal. Someone who would think I'm genuinely funny. Pretty unlikely, I know."

"You have to be exaggerating. I can't imagine your dates dashing off before the entree is served."

"It's happened three times. I don't count the fourth time because the woman excused herself to the restroom before the waiter could take our order. I never saw her again."

"That's terrible."

"It didn't do much for my ego. The hostess informed me later that she'd taken a cab. I sat waiting for her to come back for twenty-five minutes. Talk about a disaster. Do you ever wish you could hop into a good relationship, like a year into it, without enduring all those first few dates? Just avoid it completely?"

"Every day." For one breathless moment, Katherine's pulse jolted to a stop.

Was Jack trying to ask her out on a date? No, he couldn't be. His daughter despised her. But, if he wasn't, then this conversation didn't make a lot of sense. Unless it wasn't *her* he was interested in. Disappointment slid like ice into her heart. "You want me to fix you up with someone, don't you?"

"Not at all. I'm just curious how another single adult feels about the whole dating thing. Are you?"

"Am I what?"

"Going to let your sisters set you up?"

So he hadn't called because he was interested in her. She swallowed down the disappointment and tried to keep it out of her voice. "I'm considering it."

"Maybe we should make a deal. You go out on a date. I go out on a date. It would sure help me to start risking my dignity with all those inevitable first-date disasters, knowing that you were risking it, too. What do ya say?"

What she really disliked was that he was right about her. She had a hard time saying no, if it would hurt someone's feelings. And then she was in a pickle, because she didn't go back on her word, either. Spence said she was a softy, and she was. She cared. About Jack. About him finding some nice women who would value him. She cared about Hayden getting the right stepmother to improve her life.

It's already been established that can't be me. Holding herself very still, she said the only thing she honestly could. "If it would help you, Jack. Sure."

"Great." He sounded happy. Really happy.

And that's what she wanted. Even if her heart hurt so much, it seemed to stop beating. And the funny part was that she hadn't even realized how much she liked Jack. Until this moment.

"I gotta go, my hour's up and it's back to work." His smile radiated over the phone. "Thanks for the talk. I'll call you."

"Sure." It was the only word she could manage. She disconnected the line and stared down at her hands. She couldn't believe it. They were still shaking. It wasn't as if she had anything to be nervous about. Not now.

So, he wasn't interested in her, and it hurt. But that was that.

Let it rain. Jack didn't mind the cold, wet, nearly freezing temperatures. Not a bit. He settled into his cruiser, cranked over the engine and punched the defroster on high. His windshield was pure fog, so while he waited for the glass to clear he called Jonas.

"Yo, Jack. What's up?"

"I've thought it over and I'll do it. I'll go on that date. But one condition."

"There's always something. What?"

"Please. Don't tell Katherine my name or what I do. Not yet. I want it to be a surprise."

"Katherine hasn't put two and two together."

"Just make sure she doesn't, okay? I don't want to blow this. I want to do it right. I'll let her know, but I want to do it my way."

"You got it."

He disconnected, feeling hopeful. More hopeful than he'd felt in a long time. In years. In so long, that it felt like a century.

Hayden wasn't going to like this, but he felt that she'd come around in time. He couldn't think of a better role model for his daughter than Katherine. She was perfect. Just thinking about her filled his heart right up. He felt as if he'd closed his eyes and dreamed her up. She was honest and upright, faithful and good, kind and as likeable as could be. She was beautiful. He adored everything about her. Even her tendency to be super-organized.

She was too special. He wanted her in his life. More than he'd ever wanted anything for himself. With all he was and with all he had. He didn't want to think how he'd feel if this didn't work out.

All he could do was his best, and he'd trust God with the rest.

In the cold gray dawn, March was roaring like a lion, so when Katherine lowered her car window to place an order at the espresso stand, she got a face full of wind-driven ice, sleet and rain.

Great. After ordering a cinnamon mocha, she looked at herself in the visor mirror. Yikes. Talk about wind damage. *Bedraggled* wasn't the word. It couldn't be good that it was seven in the morning, and already the day wasn't going well.

It will get better, right, Lord? She wasn't

feeling too hopeful as she dug a five from her wallet. She hadn't slept well last night, high winds had woken her up and kept her awake, but the storm wasn't the only reason.

Jack. She couldn't explain why learning he wasn't interested in dating her felt like a loss, something beyond disappointment. She'd given it to God, and this was God's answer. This is how things were meant to be.

Let it go, Katherine. She took a steadying breath. Her coffee was ready, so she powered down her window, handed over the five and her punch card in exchange for the toasted bagel and the enormous cup of blistering-hot espresso. Whipped cream oozed out of the lid's drinking spout.

Excellent. She thanked the lady and left her change in the tip jar. She slid the car into gear and froze. There was a black SUV just like Jack's pulling into the lot directly toward her, aimed at the order window on the other side of the booth.

That can't be him, she told herself, so don't even look. Even if it was, she didn't know if she wanted to see him, so she kept her eyes on the road. Heart stinging, she didn't look in her rearview mirror until she'd pulled back into traffic and was heading in the direction of the store. She could see a man, window down, giving his order with a smile. Jack's face. Jack's smile.

The stinging in her heart worsened, so she kept driving through the wind and the storm, sad. Feeling so very sad.

Not quite able to let it go.

Jack felt a brush, like a whisper, that moved sweetly through him. He'd felt this before—when he was near Katherine. He looked around and only saw torrential downpour and cars he didn't recognize. Then he realized he didn't even know what she drove.

After getting hot tea for himself and a vanilla steamer for Hayden, he drove her to school, wished her a good day and felt her unhappiness to the bottom of his soul. He watched her walk away, taking more of his heart with her. Dressed in her school uniform, navy sweater and slacks, saddle shoes, she looked like the good, wholesome girl she was inside. This was his daughter. He loved her so much.

Watch over her, Lord. Please keep her safe today.

He stayed until she'd passed through the double doors into the school. Only then could he move on, negotiating the jam of traffic. He checked the time. He had a meeting with Pastor

Marin for counseling. This head stuff wasn't his thing and he wasn't comfortable with it, but he needed help. Marin had suggested Hayden was going through the stages of grief, which everyone did after a loss.

There was hope on the other side. He was banking on that.

Maybe hope for him, too.

Oh, no. The copier guy. Katherine spotted him the second she reached the doorway. The meeting room was crowded tonight, full of people, talking casually, Bibles open or closed before them, and he hadn't noticed her standing in the doorway.

Maybe he's just here for a little fellowship, she thought. *Please Lord, let him be here for his spiritual needs.*

"C'mon," Marin coaxed behind her in the hallway. "The copier guy is here, but I'll help you avoid him."

"I don't think that will help." Katherine lowered her voice, not that she was in danger of being overheard due to the amazing cacophony of sound in the hallway from all the other meeting rooms. "I have a feeling of doom."

"That's never good, but have faith. Isn't that

why you're here?" Marin grinned. She was ob-
viously enjoying this. "You'd better find a seat.
Oh, how about right here, next to the door?
You can hide from the copier guy here."

"I have the feeling you knew the copier guy
was going to be here. I thought you were on my
side."

"I'm always on your side, girlfriend." Marin
gave her a hug. "Have a little faith. Now, who
else is here besides the copier guy?"

She said that as if she was expecting someone else.

I don't even want to know, Katherine thought
and scrunched into the first available seat she
came to and scooted her chair directly behind
a much taller man. It was the closest she was
going to get to being invisible.

An icy prickle tingled at the back of her neck,
and she recognized it. She'd felt it before.

Someone settled into the chair next to her.
Jack. She didn't have to look to know it was
him. She could feel the might and personality
radiating outward from him. She recognized
the faint woodsy scent of his soap, and, of
course, a corresponding knot of anxiety coiled
to life in her midsection.

"What are you doing here?" The words popped
out of her mouth before she could stop them.

As if he hadn't noticed how horrified she'd sounded, Jack shrugged out of a rain-speckled jacket, revealing the blue on blue patrolman's uniform beneath. "It's a much smaller town than you think. What were the chances we'd both be here tonight?"

"Because I told you about the meeting?" Katherine noticed he didn't look nearly as surprised as she was to see him. "Aren't you supposed to be at work?"

"I'm taking an early dinner hour, so I can only stay for half the meeting. Is the copier guy here?"

He dazzled her, leaning close as if they were more than acquaintances, more than friends. For a moment her chest drew tight and her spirit brightened, overwhelmed by his nearness. By the warm gleam of gold and bronze in his eyes, by the manly texture of his shaved jaw, by the deep unspoken wish she felt. She wanted to know more.

Too much more. Like, was he as emotionally tender as she sensed he could be? What would it feel like to have him hold her hand, his fingers twined with hers? What would it be like to be held by him? Would it be nice and safe and sheltering?

Katherine, this is not what you should be thinking about. She took a steadying breath, willing down these out-of-place hopes. After all, she was a sensible girl. "The copier guy. Yes, he's here."

"That's why you're hiding in the back?"

"Guilty."

A friendly grin played at the corners of his mouth. A very handsome mouth. "Do you have that date lined up?"

"Date?" Why did her mind go blank when he smiled? Think, Katherine. "Oh, you mean the one—my sisters—uh, I'm going to."

"Good." Jack smiled full-on and dazzling. "I have a hunch this is the right man for you."

His words were like an arrow to her heart. Okay, there was a silver lining to this, and she'd concentrate on that. The good part was that he hadn't gotten the slightest clue that she liked him. Because if he had, she'd be too embarrassed to look him in those dazzling eyes. "I was going to call Danielle tonight when I got home. How about you?"

He nodded, his gaze sharpening on hers. Intense. The noise in the room faded to silence. The colors and lights and the presence of other people vanished. It felt as if they were alone. That the cadence of her pulse slowed to match his.

It's a good thing he didn't like her, because she'd be in trouble. It's a good thing the wish aching deep in her chest wasn't her heart longing.

Remember, you were never more than mildly interested in him, Katherine.

Not true. Her usual defense method of denial wasn't working at all. Ripping her gaze from his, she fumbled through her beloved Bible, checking the chapter and verse written on the blackboard at the front, unable to find Corinthians. Her hands were shaking so badly she couldn't turn the whisper-thin pages. What had happened to Corinthians? It was here the last time she looked.

Face it, Katherine. You're rattled. Jack was the first man she'd *really* liked in a long time. Somewhere down deep, she had to acknowledge the truth. She'd fallen for him. Truly fallen. When she looked at him, she saw the lawman strong and honorable in his uniform; but she also saw much more.

The devoted father, the lonely widower, his big honest heart, his unyielding sense of responsibility. The man who, like her, had tried to date many times, only never to have it work out. It could wear you down after a while, the disappointment of not connecting emotionally and spiritually with the right person, and fearing that you never would.

It was as if she could peer into his heart and see him. How much he cared, how much he fought to do the right thing, how hard he believed. The strength it took to lose a wife and bury her, to go on and get through for his daughter. She saw things he'd never told her about, but things she could *see* and *feel*. She'd never been able to do that with anyone. Not one single person. And why Jack?

Let it go, Katherine. She took a deep breath, willed the last of her disappointment away, and, as Marin started the meeting, bowed her head for the opening prayer.

Chapter Nine

"Ava's chocolate cream pie is way better than this." Marin dug her fork into the slice on the plate sitting in the exact middle of the booth's table. "She should sell her stuff to places like this. Have you told her that?"

"She doesn't listen to me. She thinks I don't know anything."

"All younger sisters think that of their big sisters." Marin went for another forkful of pie. "This is just what I needed. Lots of chocolate after a fourteen-hour day."

"How long before they hire a new minister?"

"Who knows? Our congregation keeps growing. This time last year, we felt over-staffed. Now Ron retires, and I'm leading adult evening groups."

Katherine dug her fork into her side of the

pie. "You knew Jack was going to be there, didn't you?"

"I mentioned the meeting to him, nothing more. He's a member of the church now."

"There are plenty of other churches in this city. Why ours?"

"Because his daughter's involved in my youth projects and I invited them. That's right before I told him all about our programs for kids and adults, including the singles' groups. Do you know what else?"

"I'm afraid to know."

"I think you like him."

"Just a little. He seems all right." That was the understatement of the millennium. Katherine made sure she got some extra whipped cream on her next forkful of pie. She needed it. She wasn't happy until a mound of chocolate oozed over the side of her fork, rich and comforting enough to make her temporarily forget. "Jack's not my type."

"Oh, of course not. A big handsome man like that wouldn't be any woman's type. Honestly." Marin stopped with her fork in midair, contemplative. "You know what else? I knew the moment I saw him leaving the ski lounge, and you were sitting there all alone. You like him and you've moved past the denial stage."

"You're totally wrong."

"And into the hesitant stage. Where you let yourself admit he's sort of all right, but you're hedging on that because you're not really interested. No big deal. Except it is a *huge* deal."

"That's because it really isn't a big deal. Jack is an okay guy but I'm not interested. It's as simple as that." And she would make sure of it. She was in control of her feelings, and it wasn't a big issue that he didn't want to date her.

"Interesting." Marin switched to a German accent, as if she were Freud. "Very interesting. Tell me more."

"How about you? What happened to that really handsome counselor you liked at the homeless shelter?" Katherine watched Marin's fork tumble from her fingers and hit the table. "So, that must mean you like him?"

"That means I'm liking him but I'm not letting him know. Just in case he does what every other man on the planet does. They are horrified and sputter a lot and make it clear they are not interested. To him, a lady minister is the same as being the reverend mother of a convent."

"They don't see you as marrying material."

"You don't have that problem. You just don't give most men a chance."

"I want it to be right, you know?" Katherine

remembered how Jack had had to leave for work, and had slid out with a smile before the refreshment part of the evening. Why did her mind just go right to Jack? She had to stop thinking about him like that. "I don't want to settle. I want the real thing."

"Speaking of which, I saw you with Cliff."

"The copier guy? Yeah. I need more chocolate for this. Wait a minute." Katherine forked straight into the pie, taking out an enormous glob of chocolate and chocolate cookie crust. After she chewed and swallowed, she was fortified enough to discuss it. "He asked me out, and I had to tell him no. It was horrible."

"There are worse things, and I know you turned him down kindly."

"I did my best, but it hurt him." She knew the feeling first-hand. "Love is a weird thing, isn't it? I think he really liked me, but I didn't feel anything for him. Zip. He was nice in every way, there just wasn't that spark. That hopeful awareness in your heart that overrides everything."

The one she had for Jack—not that she was ready to admit it. The feeling that Jack didn't have for her. "Why is it so hard to find that feeling happening for a man who actually feels that for you?"

"It's supposed to be that way. Real love is a

precious gift. You just don't find it anywhere, every day."

"True. But where does that leave us?"

"Sitting here together eating chocolate."

Katherine's cell phone rang and she plunged her hand into her purse trying to find it. "It's probably Ava. She either locked herself out of her—"

Jack Munroe. She had to blink to make sure she wasn't imagining his name on the LCD screen. Nerves gripped her stomach. "I don't *have* to take it. It'll keep."

Marin leaned over the table far enough to see the screen. She grinned as if she knew a secret. "Answer it."

"Don't say it as if he likes me. It's not that way between us. What the copier guy is to me, I am to Jack."

"Sure. He's probably just calling because he needs a friend, since he's new to the area and probably hasn't met many people yet."

New to the area? Wasn't the guy Danielle had wanted to set her up with new to the area, too? She'd never seen Jack around before Hayden's incident, but she just assumed they'd never crossed paths before. It wasn't as if she knew everyone in the city. "Hi, Jack. Did you just move here?"

"Hello to you, too." His baritone rumbled as warm as melted butter. "From Phoenix. Why?"

"I'm sitting here with Marin and she said that about you."

"What else is she saying about me?"

"Nothing good. It's sad, really."

He chuckled softly. "True. I'm a sad case. Can I ask you something?"

"Sure." Why did her heart double-beat like that, and then stop altogether? She held her feelings very still. They were friends, that's all.

"Being new to the area, I don't know one restaurant from the next. Since I'm going on this blind date, I want to pick a really fine place with excellent food. In case the woman I'm meeting doesn't like me, at least she'll have the consolation of a very nice meal."

Of course. If Katherine needed proof he didn't see her *that* way, this was it. "How pricey are you thinking?"

"Pricey. What's *your* very favorite place?"

"It's the steakhouse on County Homes Boulevard. You won't find a better filet mignon anywhere. The view of the mountains is priceless." I can't believe I'm doing this. She took a steadying breath. "If you want to make a good impression, take her there."

"I will. Thanks for the tip."

"Anytime." She disconnected and tossed her phone into her purse. It clanked into something and made a terrible sound, but she didn't care.

This was what she got for being sensible. For wearing sensible shoes. For wearing sensible clothes. For living a sensible life. She looked down at herself. She wore a navy blue blouse buttoned up to the top collar button, sleeves buttoned at the cuffs, and matching navy pleated slacks, finished with navy blue all-weather loafers, because it was raining outside.

Yep, this is me, she thought, sensible from head to toe. A few more years and *she* was going to be mistaken for a reverend mother.

"Well, there's always Cliff," Marin teased. "Poor Cliff."

Katherine studied the empty plate between them. Nothing but a few crumbs were left. She signaled for the waitress. "I'm going to need more pie."

"You seem down," Marin commented as they wandered from the mall entrance of the restaurant and stood in the wide breezeway. "Normally after two slices of chocolate cream, most people are much happier."

"It's nothing." And everything. She stared at

her image reflected in a store's windows. "I've done the dumbest thing. I agreed to go on a blind date to help Jack get the courage to go on one, too."

"You mean, together? That's awesome. I knew—"

"No, separately. A friend of his wants to fix him up. And so when I blabbed that Danielle wanted to set me up, he said he'd go on his, if I'd go on mine. And now I have to say yes to a blind date."

"You like Jack. That's why you couldn't say no to him."

"I only sort of like him, and not like *that*." Because I refuse to let it be. She took another steadying breath. It wasn't easy keeping so many emotions stuffed down inside.

Marin stood beside her, staring at their reflections, nice wholesome women in very sensible clothes. Unlike the dressed mannequins in the window display, who looked trendy.

Katherine sighed again, burdened by her disposition in life. "I could never look stylish, no matter what I wore. If I dressed up in a pink suede little skirt like that, I'd just look like I was trying to be something I wasn't."

"I don't have the narrow hips for anything

trendy. The Polish side of the family is very hippy. I take after them." Marin sighed. "Not only that, my hair gets thin when it gets too long. The Swedish side of the family is half bald. Don't laugh. My gene pool could be better. Do you know what I need? To get my hair trimmed."

Katherine considered her own hair. She'd had this same exact style since she was nine. Straight bangs across her forehead and long hair straight to her mid-shoulder. "There's a salon in the mall. Want to go see if they have any openings?"

"Absolutely. C'mon." Marin took off and screeched to a halt, considered the direction and pointed left. "This way."

When Katherine was pivoting to keep up with her, she caught something in her peripheral vision. Not something—someone. There was a teenage girl, average height, and average build with blondish hair styled like Hayden's and wearing a black jacket. She froze in place. That wasn't Hayden, was it?

The teenager was out of sight, gone perhaps into one of the many stores still open. She waited a beat, trying to decide if she'd imagined it. A girl appeared from a store, average height, average build, but her hair was more brown than blond and wearing a black jacket. Definitely not Hayden.

"What?" Marin asked. "Did you see someone you know?"

"No, I just thought I did. I was mistaken." Surely Hayden was home on a school night, doing homework.

The problem was her, all her. Katherine had Jack Munroe on her mind. And that was wrong, wrong, wrong. She followed Marin into the salon and, since there was only one technician free for a walk-in, Katherine let Marin go first. She could wait. After all, she only needed the lightest of trims. It would take all of five minutes, tops.

She was the only one sitting in the waiting area with a perfect view of the wide mall corridors. A couple sauntered by, side by side and hand in hand. It was the way the man watched his wife that made Katherine ache with longing. She wanted to be cherished like that.

She had to be practical. She was over thirty. Somehow, the years just kept ticking by and every year that passed felt empty. She had family and friends and a job she liked. A home she felt cozy in. Hobbies that kept her happy and fulfilled.

But in the long hours in the evening, when

her condo felt lonely, empty and echoing around her, she had to admit it wasn't enough. Life was passing her by because she had no sincere, responsible mountain of a man to love and no children to give all the unused affection in her heart.

What if this man Danielle wanted to fix her up with was The One? Surely it was worth the risk to find out, right? What was she losing besides a little time out of an evening?

Don't answer that. Katherine fished her phone out of her purse and hit the speed dial, fully knowing that she was being way too optimistic. What if it was another uncomfortable, lots-of-awkward-silences blind date? There were worse things in the universe.

"Hi, Katherine," Jonas answered over the sound of a bawling baby. "Madison is cutting another tooth. Sorry for the decibel level. Dani is in helping Tyler with his bath. Let me get the door open and I'll hand you over to her."

There was lots of background noise and Madison's crying eased. Danielle came onto the phone. "Katherine? It's wild and wooly here. Have you thought about the date?"

"I have to know something first. He's a nice guy, right? You're sure about it?"

"After what you've been through, you can

bank on it. This man is a complete gentleman. Do you want to meet him?"

"Oh, just set me up. I've been on blind dates before and survived with most of my dignity intact. Probably I can do it again."

"That's the spirit."

So why, Katherine wondered, did she feel even more depressed when she hung up? Because she was hoping that dating someone else—someone she hoped she would like— would be the best way to move past this impossible crush she had on Jack Munroe.

Jack was too dog-tired to wonder if this was a divine intervention or simply coincidence. He only knew he was glad. He hardly noticed the arctic windchill or the puddles of rainwater he had to splash through to get from his cruiser to the sensible beige sedan pulled over on the highway's wide shoulder. Whatever reason, it was his lucky day.

Katherine McKaslin, her shocked face revealed as her driver's-side window zipped down, obviously didn't know what to think, either. The wind whipped at the ends of her light blond hair. "Jack?"

"Wow. You cut your hair."

"I'm surprised you recognized me. My

family is going to flip. I was driving along with hair-cutter's remorse and I wasn't paying attention to my speedometer. Usually I never speed. How fast was I going?" She bit her bottom lip, sure she was in trouble.

"Enough that I'm gonna have to cuff you and haul you down to the station."

"*What?* You're kidding, right?"

Cute. She was real cute. "Right. In fact, you weren't speeding at all. You have a taillight out."

"Really? Oh. Okay." She reached behind her passenger's side visor where an organizer was attached and quickly extracted her registration and proof of insurance. "Let me get my license. How much is that going to cost me?"

Was it his imagination or was she rattled, and not because she thought she was facing a ticket, either. She fumbled through her neatly organized wallet and when she withdrew her license, she dropped it. It tumbled out of sight.

Now, there *could* be another explanation to her nervousness. His chest fluttered. "Knowing you, the taillight probably konked out about five minutes ago. I won't even give you a warning. I know you'll get it fixed."

"First thing."

Yeah, he knew.

There wasn't much traffic on the highway this time of evening—well, compared to a big metropolitan area, there wasn't much traffic ever. But for Bozeman standards, it was a very light night. The storm was keeping most people off the roads.

He waited for a triple-trailer semi to whoosh by, going slowly due to the weather conditions. Jack did a visual of lights and plates before turning back to Katherine. He liked her new cut, the way the bobbed ends of gold curled in to frame her chin, emphasizing the oval shape of her face.

Definitely lovely.

The flutter in his chest sped up a notch. "How did it work out with the copier guy?"

"You're the fourth person to ask that tonight. First Marin, then my sisters. There's nothing going on. He asked me for a date and I declined."

"Do you do that a lot?"

"What? Turn down dating opportunities? Mostly I'm pretty picky. I have to know a man first, you know, like with Kevin, my fiancé—"

"I didn't know you'd been engaged."

Her voice thinned with pain. "A few years ago, but it didn't work out."

Why? he wondered. Why would any man ever let her go?

"Anyway, Kevin and I went to the same church all of our lives. We went to the same schools. While I didn't know him closely, I knew that he wasn't the kind of man who would harm a woman, or deceive her in any way."

"It sounds smart. I've seen a lot of horrible stuff through the years. Most shifts are like this, quiet, helping with minor problems, broken-down cars or patrolling. But sometimes I see what some people can be capable of. It's not a safe world. It's good to be cautious."

"Cautious is my middle name."

He liked that about her, that she was careful and conscientious and sensible. She was the kind of woman a man could count on. All sorts of protective feelings rose to the surface, and it wasn't easy for a man like him to deal with. He liked things cut and dry, emotions under control.

He had a feeling that was a sign in itself. No one had ever made him come alive, soul-deep, like Katherine did. "Will I see you when I drop Hayden off after school? Or will you be busy in your office again?"

"Probably the office. There's this financial thing Spence is all worked up about."

"Then I guess I'll see you at church." He tipped his hat. "Drive safe, Katherine."

"You too, Jack." Her window zipped up, camouflaging her behind the glass.

Only as he backed away did the utter wetness of the rain begin to register and the bitter cut of the wind. With every step he took, he became wetter and colder. Lonelier, when she drove away on the dark ribbon of highway. He felt as empty as that lonely stretch of road.

He wasn't falling for Katherine; he'd already fallen. It was a done deal. But he couldn't stomach the possibility that she might not feel the same way.

Chapter Ten

"*What did you do to your hair?*"

Katherine swiveled away from her computer monitor to see Danielle in her office doorway, with little Madison on one hip. Gladness uplifted her as she abandoned her work and scooped her grumpy niece into her arms. "She's still cutting that tooth?"

"It's not easy being little." Danielle looked exhausted, but her voice and her smile were loving as she hitched the diaper bag into a better place on her shoulder. "I can't believe this. I'm sorry, but…I'm in shock. I hardly recognize you."

"You and everybody else I've seen today." Katherine tried not to let it bother her. This is what happened when a girl acted rashly and didn't think things through. And now it was too late, she had to live with it.

"I was in the mood for something different, what can I say?" She circled around the corner of her desk to the seating area near the wide window, giving her niece a kiss on the cheek.

Madison scrunched up her cherub's face, fisted her hand and started crying. She buried her face in Katherine's blouse and sobbed, shaking.

Poor sweetie. Katherine cuddled the little one, and her heart squeezed tight. As much as she loved her precious niece, it was always a bittersweet thing to hold a baby. Always a reminder of what was best left buried in the past.

"We were up most of the night." Danielle plopped into the second chair. "We're on our way to the doctor, I'm afraid she's getting an ear infection or something because she's cut teeth before and this just isn't right."

"She feels a little warm."

"She is. But I figured if we didn't stop by now, by the time we wait for the doctor and stop to fill a prescription and pick Tyler up from the church's preschool, we'd never get a chance to do it. I have the information right here—" She opened her diaper bag, pulled out her purse and rifled through it. "Somewhere."

"What information? Oh, right. The blind date guy."

"Yep. Here it is." She flipped open her date book. "How does Saturday night work for you? I know you usually close the store early on Saturdays, right?"

In truth, no day would be good, but since she had to do this, it might as well be Saturday. "Sure."

"That's not a very enthusiastic sure."

"It's the best I can manage. What's this man's name and where am I meeting him?"

"I think he wanted to pick you up."

"No. I'm not going anywhere with a stranger, and you know why, Danielle." She shook her head, willing the painful thoughts out of her mind before they set in, as they used to do with such force. "I meet him at the restaurant, or no deal."

"Okay. I'll tell him that. It's just that—" She slipped her book back into her purse and the purse back into the diaper bag. "He's not a stranger to Jonas and he's one of the good ones. You have my word on it."

"I still won't do it."

"Okay, I'll tell Jonas and he can get the where and the when. Are you sure you're all right?"

"Why wouldn't I be?" She pressed a kiss into the soft crown of Madison's curly brown hair; she was quieting. "I'm fine. Spence and I are pretty stressed about the operating budget, but we'll figure it out."

"I wasn't asking about the store. Why did you cut your hair? It looks great, but it's pretty extreme for you. What's going on?"

"Just feeling dull, I guess."

"Don't we all." Danielle sighed. "I feel less dull when I get a full night's sleep. But why you? You are so on top of everything. Is this about the roses guy?"

Jack. Why did Dani have to bring him up? Katherine had gotten through the last few hours of work without thinking of him once…since lunchtime. Every time she thought about him it was like a cut to her heart. Why had she fallen so hard and fast for him? And it was all one-sided, all her.

She cleared the emotion from her throat, refusing to let anything show. A girl had her pride, after all. "There's nothing going on with the roses guy."

A knock at her open doorway interrupted her. Spence, imposing in a black shirt and slacks, glared in, dourly. "Sorry. Did you know the copier isn't working? I went to use it and nothing. Give the repair guy a call, okay? Oh, and that teenager is here. Since Ava isn't, you deal with her. I don't have time."

Katherine watched her brother march off.

Dani took Madison back. "He's so Heath-cliff."

Katherine loved her brother, but he wasn't the warm and fuzzy type. "I'd better go deal with Hayden."

Dani settled her baby daughter on her hip. "Where's Ava? Isn't she supposed to be working here?"

"Well, only because we're family and we can't fire her." It was an old joke, and an affectionate one. "She's temping last minute as a pastry chef at the big hotel downtown. It's a good opportunity. Keep her in prayer, okay? This could work into a full-time job."

"Wouldn't that be good." Dani wiped a tear from Madison's chubby cheek and kissed her forehead. "We have to go, but I'll give you a call later. I'll get the 411 for Friday night."

"And let me know what the doctor says about Madison."

Dani said goodbye and hurried out the door. Katherine meant to follow her but her intercom buzzed. She changed directions and grabbed the phone. "I'm going to have Kelly make the call, Spence. Stop stressing."

"Fine. It's the girl. I don't want her unsupervised in this store. Kelly's ringing up a sale, and

I'm too busy to watch her. You let her back in this store. You deal with her." He disconnected with a terse click.

Fine. The money situation was really getting to Spence. He felt his responsibility to their parents so strongly. His heart was in the right place, but... She stepped wide of his office door and found Hayden slouched in a chair in the sitting area meant for customers.

The teenager radiated the attitude of a secular hip-hop singer while wearing her wholesome navy blue school uniform of an oxford shirt and pleated trousers.

Hayden didn't look happy. Anger glittered in her eyes. It wasn't hard to see what lay beneath. Pain. Fear. Sadness.

Yeah, she knew what that was like, too. "Hayden, come with me and we'll get you started on the March mailing."

"Whatever." Hayden drew herself up out of the chair with a protesting snort.

Katherine wasn't bothered by it. She pulled a box of newsletters from a shelf beneath the front counter and a box of business-sized envelopes. "Kelly's already folded and stuffed a box full." She set that box on the end of the counter for Hayden. "Your job is to seal the envelope and adhere the mailing label."

Hayden grabbed an envelope. "I know you like my dad and everything. But he's only being nice to you because you didn't press charges. That's the only reason. Just so you know."

Not sure what she should say to that, Katherine opted for silence. She hesitated at her office doorway, glancing over her shoulder one more time. There was no missing the satisfied smirk on the girl's face.

Katherine went to her desk. Since she could see Hayden through the open doorway, she made sure to keep an eye on her.

It had to be a sign, Katherine thought, from heaven above. A call from Dani confirmed it. She was calling from the waiting room at the doctor's office. She said the blind-date guy would be willing to meet her Saturday night. The steakhouse on Country Homes Boulevard. Seven o'clock.

Katherine jotted it down on her day timer. Then it struck her. That was the restaurant she'd recommended to Jack. Surely he wasn't the blind date? No, that's just wishful thinking, Katherine. Her gaze cut to Hayden, head down, jaw set, frown in place, sealing envelope after envelope.

No, there's just no way. I have to let this go. She flipped her diary to the current day's page and banished Jack Munroe from her mind. But he remained in her heart like a weight so heavy, it felt as if not even prayer could remove it.

"I can't get used to your haircut."

Katherine watched Ava lean across the kitchen counter, where she was sitting in her yoga outfit, reaching for the cookie jar. "I just wanted to get out of a rut."

"That's why I avoid ruts entirely. Once you get in one, it's tough to get out. Right, Aubrey?"

"Totally."

Katherine checked the chicken simmering on the stove—it was done—and lifted the skillet onto a back burner. "Why do I get the feeling you're no longer employed?"

"Hey, this time it wasn't anything I did. It was just a one-day deal. Lindsay, you know, she's the head chef, we went to school together. She said it was only a one-day thing, their pastry chef had a wedding to go to. But—"

"This means you need more hours at the bookstore?" Katherine guessed as she gave the brown rice a stir.

Ava plucked the lid off the ceramic jar and began transferring custard-filled iced cookies into the beehive. "I also have good news. One of the bakeries messed up on Kristy Brisbane's wedding-cake order, and she asked if I would do it for her. Kind of a last-minute thing."

"That's great, Ava. Isn't this, what, the third or fourth time this has happened lately? You might be able to turn it into a business."

"Don't scare me like that. Aubrey, what do you think?"

"You'd have to be responsible. And not set your own kitchen on fire."

"Problems I need to work on."

The phone rang. Perfect timing. Katherine was draining the green beans. "Aubrey, would you get that?"

"My pleasure." Aubrey grabbed the cordless and disappeared around the corner.

That can't be good. Katherine righted the saucepan, removed the lid and plunked the pan on a waiting trivet. "Aubrey, who is it?"

"It's the white-roses guy," Ava said, giving the cookie jar a shove back into place. "I can tell."

"It better not be. It can't be." There was no reason for Jack to call, right? Still, if it was, what was Aubrey saying to him? Whatever it was, it couldn't be good. She stalked around the corner into the living room and yanked the phone out of Aubrey's hand. Just to be safe. "Hello?"

"I was just having a conversation with another one of your sisters. How many do you have?"

"Too many. Don't ask." Katherine noticed the twins were standing side by side spying on her and turned her back to them. "Wait, I know why you're calling. It's about the taillight. I got it fixed right away, just like I promised."

"I wasn't worried about it."

Okay, so why was he calling? "I can hear noise in the background. Are you on your dinner break?"

"Guilty. The diner's noisy tonight. I need help."

Katherine glanced back at her sisters, who seemed to be expecting a romance to blossom at any moment between her and Jack, when nothing could be farther from the truth. She sat in the bay window seat, the farthest point away from the twins, and kept her voice low. "Is it about your date?"

"Sure is. I've got the place figured out and made the reservations."

"For which night?"

Tea sloshed over the cup rim, scorching his fingers. Jack nearly dropped it into the saucer, making a bigger mess. She hadn't figured it out, had she? "This weekend. I'm nervous. I'd feel better if I could run some things by you. Get a woman's opinion."

"On what?"

Relief washed through him. He wanted this to go right. It was in God's hands, but after a lot of prayer, Jack had a gut feeling. This was going to work out right. "Where do women stand on flowers on the first date? Does it look like the guy's trying too hard?"

"Flowers are always a thoughtful gesture."

"Duly noted. Roses or one of those mixed bouquets?"

"Depends on the message you want to send, I guess. You're asking the wrong person, Jack. I'm not an authority on this."

"You're a woman and I need a woman's opinion. I also called to find out about your plans with the blind-date guy. You're not going to back out, right?"

"A promise is a promise. I'm meeting him tomorrow at my favorite steakhouse."

"What do you know about this guy?"

Not enough. Katherine opened the mini blind, drew her legs up and crossed them and stared out at the dark windy night. "My sister has been evasive on that information. I suspect it's someone from our church and if she told me his first name, then I'd be able to guess his identity and, foreseeing disaster, I would cancel."

"No canceling. So, what time are you meeting him?"

"At seven."

"I'll be there around that time. I tell you what, if things don't go well, how about we meet afterwards at nine for tea."

"Add a consolation dessert, and you're on." Something was troubling her, but she couldn't figure out what. Maybe she'd better not examine it too closely. She was moving on, leaving her feelings for Jack behind. Maybe this new date dude would be The One. Hey, it *could* happen.

"Thanks for the help. I'll let you go. Maybe I'll see you tomorrow night."

"Okay." She disconnected and stared at the phone.

There was so much she hadn't said to him. So much that only occurred to her now. Like how she hoped this worked out for him. That he liked this woman, and that Hayden would, too.

Remembering the quiet, confused and hurting teenager who'd worked two solid hours on the March mailing without complaint, keeping her distance, Katherine bowed her head, pushed her feelings aside and prayed. *Please let this work out for Jack and Hayden, Lord. They both deserve to be happy.*

As for her hopes? She would trust the Lord with that. Maybe that was the mistake she'd made with Kevin. She hadn't listened to God closely enough.

When she looked up the twins were still watching her. "Dinner's ready," Ava said.

Something was still bothering Katherine hours later, after she'd cleaned up the kitchen and was alone in her living room. The television wasn't holding her attention, and neither was the book she was reading. It was useless. She couldn't concentrate. Something was *definitely* bugging her.

She grabbed the phone and dialed Danielle. "I have to know something," she said the second Dani answered. "What is this guy's name?"

"I… Hold on." Either she was being evasive or she was busy. Probably busy.

I should have asked about Madison first, Katherine knew, but this date thing was fishy.

When Danielle came back on the line, she sounded busy…or evasive. "I've got to go. Jonas had to go back in, some fatality on a county road and—"

"Wait a minute. Jonas is a desk sergeant. For the state." Why hadn't she thought of that sooner? Because thoughts of Jack had distracted her, that's why. "Does this guy work with him? Or is he a friend?"

"Madison needs me to rock her to sleep. I was going to call you, it's a mild ear infection, nothing serious, and that's good news, right? I'll call you tomorrow."

"Tomorrow will be too late. The blind date guy isn't Jack, by chance, right?"

"I've got to go." Dani disconnected.

Either something was really wrong at home, or Danielle's evasion was a telltale sign. What if she was right? Katherine stared at the phone in her hand. Nerves attacked her stomach. What if she really did have a date with Jack tomorrow? No, don't even go there. Why wouldn't he have just asked her out if he was interested in dating her?

Because she would have turned him down flat, because of the way Hayden had reacted and the fact that Jack hadn't seemed interested in her. He'd only been a friend.

Well, unless she didn't count the *quite a lady* comment.

No, it couldn't be him. It just couldn't be. She wasn't going to get her hopes raised only to have them broken. Be practical, Katherine. A date the same night, reservations around the same time at the same restaurant, those things were only a coincidence.

Unless maybe he was trying to romance her. She thought about their recent talks. They'd had a lot of conversations centering around making this blind date of his a successful one and the kind of a man she was looking for.

Maybe Jack really was asking her opinion, but maybe…

Oh, her hopes were already sky-high. She could feel them soaring despite every bit of her willpower to hold them down.

She was surprised by how much she wanted this. *If* it were true.

She headed down the hall and into her walk-in closet, to go through her wardrobe. She'd wear something nice, something complementary and not too dull.

Just in case.

Jack got in after dawn, dog-tired from a long hard shift. Nothing new about that. He'd spent an hour on his own time sitting in the hospital with a young newlywed involved in a car accident, while she waited to find out if her husband would pull through.

She had seemed so young at nineteen; Hayden would be that age in a few years. He'd stayed until her mom had arrived from Great Falls and the news had been delivered by the surgeon, her husband would make it.

Mrs. Garcia was up, bustling around the kitchen, tea water rumbling on a back burner. "I have breakfast all cooked and keeping warm in the oven. I'll be back tonight."

She grabbed her purse and coat, buttoned herself into it and headed out the back door. This wasn't the way he'd hoped to start his day, but long hours were part of the job. He'd get Hayden to the shelter, come home and get what sleep he could. Tonight was the big night. He'd find out for sure how Katherine felt about him.

Please, Lord, I'm hoping for this. He rubbed at the sudden, sharp-edged pain in his chest. It was just his heart, longing. He'd given it up to the Lord, but it wasn't easy. Waiting. Planning. Taking the steps and the risks to see if this was the right path.

Or not.

He took the stairs slow, heading down the hall, and knocked on Hayden's door. Nothing. "Hope you're up and dressed. We've got just enough time for breakfast. Marin's expecting you at eight."

The door swung open and there she was, dressed in a Phoenix Suns sweatshirt and a pair of worn jeans. "I'm not going, so there. I've done enough. I don't wanna work at that gross shelter."

"This is your last day there. I know you don't like it, but work hard and the time will go faster. You'll be done and having fun at Marin's pizza party before you know it."

"I guess."

Genuine tears stood in her eyes, and sympathy filled him. She'd had such a hard time. There was no doubt about that, and that she'd had little say in some of the tough things that had happened in their lives. He didn't either. "I know. But do it anyway. It's important that you do this."

"You could talk to *Katherine*." She dragged out the name with distaste. "She likes you."

"And I like her. She's a pretty nice lady. I want you to like her, too."

Hayden crossed her arms in front of her like a shield. "If I do, we could talk to her. Get her to forget this whole thing."

"I'm not going to do that, kiddo."

"Pleease?"

"Do you know why I want you to spend time around women like Katherine and Marin? Because they are good role models for you. And I like Katherine very much."

Hayden's jaw went rigid.

Yeah, he knew she didn't like that. "You stole from Katherine's family. People who work hard for their living, just like I do. I want you to understand how valuable hard work is and learn some respect for it now, before you make bigger mistakes you can't fix as easily."

"But, Daddy, I'm like slave labor, and that's *illegal.*"

"And the shoplifting? What about that? How can you undo that so none of this other stuff is necessary?"

She wrenched away. "I can't." Her words were muffled, on the edge of tears.

"That's part of being a grown-up. Knowing that your actions can't be taken back. That what you do and say, believe and decide all have consequences. Long-lasting ones."

"I don't need a lecture, Daddy."

He knew what she'd left unsaid. That she needed her mother.

He pulled Hayden against him and let her cry. She'd done so little of it after Heidi's death. It was so easy to keep things bottled up inside, he knew. His daughter took after him, too.

Chapter Eleven

Katherine's entire cardio-pulmonary system stopped when her doorbell rang. Why, it made no sense. It wasn't as if she would find her date at the door. They were meeting at the restaurant, right? Her sisters never rang the bell. They would have used their keys and walked right in.

She dropped her hairbrush on her dresser and hurried through the condo, shoeless, her nylons rustling. She saw the delivery van through her living-room window. A floral delivery van.

Her spirits lifted. She knew just what she could find when she pulled open the door. A bouquet of two dozen white rosebuds, pearl-white and perfect. The deliveryman was a member of their church. "Hi, Mike."

"Hi, Katherine. Where do you want this?"

"On the entry table is fine. Did Sarah do the arrangement?"

"Yep, my wife has a real talent."

"She does. Thank her for me. It's beautiful." She tugged a small side drawer from the console table where she kept a stack of ones for tipping the pizza driver and counted out a few for Mike. "Is there a card so I know who sent them?"

"Nope. No card." He grinned as he pocketed the ones on his way out the door. "It's a mystery."

Joy started in her heart and spread outward like sunshine until she glowed. Jack. It wasn't such a mystery. She inhaled the delicate rose scent and caught her reflection in the mirror. Her new haircut made her look so different, she still didn't recognize herself.

She'd chosen a teal silk pants set, dressy enough for a fine restaurant but modest and feminine all at once. She liked the color, more vibrant than she usually wore. It had been hidden in her closet for at least six months, an impulsive purchase. She'd never had the confidence to wear such a bold color. She looked okay, but no new hairstyle or fashionable clothes could change the fact that it was just her. Just Katherine.

She didn't have the best of luck when it came to first dates. And blind dates? Disaster. Nerves skittered through her midsection. She wanted this date to go well. *A little help, Lord. I hope tonight won't be a catastrophe of major proportions.*

She placed her hand over her heart. She'd already been up and down over this man. And here she was, nervous and hoping and happy. Wondering *if*. If things went well tonight, would there be more dates? If he was serious… he had to be, he'd asked all those questions. If he were the man she thought he was…only time would truly tell. If, in time, he would love her enough to look past the wounds in her life, the ones that Kevin could not?

So much uncertainty. She wasn't good at uncertainty. Hence the engagement diary, the organized kitchen cabinets and linen shelves, the neat and tidy desk, the scheduled, orderly life. Nerves rattled through her. She'd never been so nervous over a date before. It was proof of how important this was to her—more than she wanted to admit to herself, but there was no hiding it.

I truly care about this man. Way too much for her sense of safety. What she needed to do was to take a deep breath, calm down and find her shoes. It was only six o'clock, she had an hour before she had to meet Jack, but knowing her dating luck, anything could happen. What she felt for him was too important to take chances with.

She'd taken two steps down the hallway when the phone rang, which meant she had to retrace her steps to the living room extension. The ID screen made her smile, really smile, and she felt as bright as the sun. "Hi, Jack. Thank you."

"So, you got the roses, huh?"

"Yeah, whoever this blind date guy is, he's fairly thoughtful."

"He's making a fine first impression, is he?"

"Passable."

Soft laughter. "I'm sitting at the curb in front of your condo. Do you think, since we're not strangers, that you'd let me give you a ride to the restaurant?"

"I'll be out in a minute." She managed to drop the phone only once as she was hanging up. A quick glance through the window confirmed a black SUV sitting parallel to the sidewalk with Jack inside. More nerves jolted through her with the force of a lightning bolt.

It's going to be okay. She willed down both the anxiety and the happiness. As she went in search of the right shoes, she told herself it was best to stay neutral, just in case all those ifs she'd wondered about weren't meant to be. She'd gotten used to disappointment in dating. In relationships, in general. That wasn't how she wanted it to be.

What had happened to her shoes? She found them in the closet where they were supposed to be. It took just a moment to slip her feet into them and stop in front of the mirror.

Positive thoughts, Katherine. Nothing's going to go wrong. It's going to be a wonderful date. Right? If she felt a flicker of foreboding in her stomach, she attributed it to nerves. She grabbed her purse and jacket, lifted her keys from the hooked organizer in the kitchen and locked the deadbolt after her.

There was Jack, leaning against the passenger door of the SUV, hands jammed into the pockets of his black overcoat, fine-looking in a black shirt and tie and slacks. Wow. He gave her a look, definitely not a 'we're just friends' look. This one said he thought she was wow, too, in a respectful way.

But an interested way.

He opened the passenger door for her. "You look beautiful."

"Thank you. You look nice, too." She brushed past him to settle into the comfortable leather seat, willing her heart and her nerves to calm down.

"I hope you don't mind getting there early. I wanted to make sure to allow for any minor disasters, not that there will be any. I just want to be prepared."

"A good motto for those of us who are disaster-prone."

"Why, are you planning on ditching me after the entree?"

"I'm wearing heels, and they're pretty high ones for me. Not the best running shoes."

"Good to know." His grin widened to an arresting smile.

The door closed and she watched him circle around the front of the vehicle. I must be hallucinating, she thought, because it's going so well. Okay, it was only two minutes into the date, but it was still a good sign, right?

The driver's-side door whipped open and there was Jack, stealing every bit of oxygen in the passenger compartment. To her, his presence was that powerful.

I'm in so much trouble if this doesn't work out, she thought, fastening her seatbelt.

Rain broke from a partly cloudy sky, speckling the windshield.

"It's just a little rain," Jack said as he started

the engine. But he was thinking, please, let it be only a little rain. He had Katherine buckled in beside him, so lovely she made his teeth ache, and he couldn't stop the rising wave of devotion crashing through him like a flash flood.

He put the SUV in gear and pulled away from the curb. He still couldn't quite believe it. He was on a date with Katherine. She'd agreed to come with him. Not only had she agreed, but she also looked happy about it. Talk about his lucky day. Jack had been prepared for flat-out disappointment when he'd dialed her number. When she'd answered, knowing he was her blind date, she'd sounded pleased.

This was so much better than the rejection he'd braced himself for. Still, the evening was early; he might as well remind her of that up front. "I've never been on a first date that didn't have some kind of disaster, so in that spirit, I have to tell you. Chances are, something's gonna go wrong tonight. I'm praying it isn't too major."

"I'm thinking positively."

"Thinking isn't enough. You're with me, Katherine. You gotta learn. Prayer is the only hope—and divine intervention. Otherwise, disaster is an iron-clad guarantee."

That made her smile, really smile, with her whole face and all the warmth of her heart. "Let's just take it a step at a time. The road is clear, there's hardly any traffic. There's no tornado warning, just a few drops of rain."

"I didn't know you were such a perky and optimistic type."

"You're leaving the sole burden of positive thinking to me and that's a scary thought. I'm struggling as it is."

He felt his heart turn inside out. A worse sign than any physical catastrophe that could happen. He slowed to a stop, waiting for a red light; they were the only ones at the intersection. "Okay, positive thoughts. We'll lighten the mood. Tell me the funniest thing that happened on a first date."

She relaxed back into the seat while they waited for the light to change. "My cousin set me up with a friend of his. In fact, he's some kind of manager at the steakhouse. Maybe we'll see him tonight. Through the entire date, he kept calling me Caroline. I kept saying to him, 'No, I'm Katherine McKaslin.' And he would interrupt me and say, 'Oh, that *awful* Katherine McKaslin.' And then I'd say, 'But *I'm* Katherine McKaslin,' and he'd say, 'Caroline, I don't want to talk about her.' This went on and on. Finally I gave up trying to explain."

"Did he ever figure it out?"

"No. He wasn't a very good listener, apparently. He called me up a few days later and said, 'Caroline, would you like to go to church with me?' I turned him down."

"Surprising. Did you ever figure out why he thought you were awful?" Because in his opinion, she was nothing less than perfect.

"I think he confused me with one of my cousins. That was the only explanation I could come up with. I mean, this man didn't know me."

Jack knew he was staring, but he couldn't help it. She was so fine…so perfect. There was that word again. How was it possible that he could fall even harder for her?

"Uh, Jack? The light's green."

Good going, Jack.

He headed into the intersection, watching the rain pound down a little harder. Wind gusted through the tall trees siding the road. Old maples that were a good thirty feet or more. He kept a sharp eye out for falling limbs. He wasn't taking any chances. He had this one shot tonight, and he wasn't going to blow it.

If Katherine didn't enjoy the evening, if she

didn't feel cared for and safe, then he'd be like the steakhouse guy. Out of luck for date number two.

Talk about pressure.

"Okay, I told you mine," she said. "You tell me your funniest first date."

"Third place would go to the woman who stole my car." Since they'd gone another quarter mile without mishap, he relaxed some. "We were driving to this great Tex-Mex place and on the way there we came on an accident. One of the injured passengers had called on her cell, but no officers had responded yet. I helped with what initial care I could until the EMTs showed up. I turned around and my Lexus was gone. It couldn't have been more than four minutes, tops, from the time I pulled over at the accident site."

"Was she mad at you for waiting, or did she really steal it?"

"She stole it. Apparently, the fact that I was a cop didn't stop her." A half mile to go, he thought, and still no disaster. It looked like smooth sailing ahead. So what if the rain was turning torrential? This was Montana, not Arizona. They didn't have monsoons and flash floods.

He relaxed some more. "The second funniest date I ever went on was—"

An explosion boomed like gunfire and rocked the vehicle. The SUV listed to the side and the telltale thud, thud, thud jolted through every inch of steel chassis. He pulled to a stop on the shoulder. "So much for positive thoughts."

"And prayers." Her gaze locked on his with a sincere apology. "I think you have a flat tire. As far as disasters go, it's not too bad. Except for the rain."

"Exactly." Jack steeled himself. Katherine was right. This wasn't even a blip on his radar. "I've got a spare. It's no big deal to change a tire. It'll take a few minutes and believe this or not, we should still get to the restaurant early. Can I plan, or what?"

"You're good, Jack. Did you want me to help?"

She was kidding, right? Not on his life. "You stay here. I'm the man. It's my job."

Katherine just smiled at him and wisely didn't say anything else, like how she'd taken a car-repair class for women that covered the basics, for safety reasons. The heavens chose to open up at the exact moment Jack stepped out of the vehicle, the poor man.

Lightning stroked through the sky above and thunder crashed so hard, the SUV rattled from the shock wave. Icy cold poured through the back when Jack opened up. Poor guy. Already he was drenched, but he was a man who handled mild disaster well. He still had a grin on his face and there wasn't a trace of stress in his voice.

"I must have run over some nails or something in the road. Both the front and back tires on my side are flat. It'll take a few minutes longer than I projected, but we'll still make our reservation." He had to shout to be heard over the deafening rain hammering down like hail.

"You think of everything."

"I try." He lifted up the back carpet and froze. The smile drained from his face. "Uh-oh. Two flat tires. But I've only got one spare. I'd consider driving on the rims, but we'd never make it. The closest building is half a mile away and it's the restaurant."

She unzipped the side compartment on her purse and hauled out her cell. "I'll call one of the tow services. Ask them to bring a tire."

"I got mine," he said, managing a half grin, not defeated yet as he reached into his coat pocket and pulled out his cell. "I'll just call Darryl over at his garage…" He stopped and stared at his screen. "No reception. Must be in a dead zone."

"Of course we are." Katherine flipped her phone on, too, thinking maybe, by some luck of the cell phone waves, she had reception. Nothing. "We can walk."

"Are you kidding? You'll get soaked. You'll get cold. Besides, I will *not* let this date turn into a disaster." At that moment lightning flared. Sparks exploded from a telephone pole half a block ahead. Thunder detonated like cluster bomb. "On second thought, maybe I'll get in and wait for this to pass over us."

"Good idea." She felt much better when Jack was in his seat, dripping rainwater like a wet dog.

Poor man. He was still half smiling, though. There was a silver lining. It was good to know just how a man you were dating handled it when things didn't go as planned. She was surprised he was as flexible as he was; she wasn't surprised he was as capable. His broad shoulders were as straight as ever.

Lightning blinded them. Instantaneous thunder hit with a force that rocked the SUV. Rain turned to hail, hitting with jackhammer force.

"This is a fun date so far, don't you think?" Jack quipped.

"It's certainly unique."

His grin turned into a full-fledged smile,

making dimples dig into his lean cheeks and those laugh lines crinkle handsomely in the corners of his eyes. "The storm's moving behind us. I'm going to jog up the road a ways and try to get reception. You aren't going to run off on me?"

"Unlike some women, I never run off until after dessert."

He laughed softly. "That's a relief. And I know you can't drive off with the car."

She laughed, too, and he was gone, jogging off through the downpour. There, a big substantial man, and then the veil of hail closed around him and he disappeared.

She'd never felt so sorely alone. Things were not going well, but it didn't seem so bad. Because it wasn't the string of unfortunate events that mattered, not compared to the feeling of simply being with him. It was like a fire crackling in a fireplace at night. Like being home, safe and warm, and glad to be there. Being with him was easier now that her nerves had faded. She really liked how he handled problems, how he tended toward humor, how he made her soul feel bright.

When he ran back into sight, even more drenched and bedraggled, gladness filled her. She'd officially moved out of the hesitant stage and landed with both feet into the uh-oh phase. She couldn't stop her heart from opening right up, hopes and fears and worries and everything exposed. Almost completely vulnerable.

This was not a sensible phase to be in. Not sensible at all. It was all feeling, all heart, and when he smiled at her and opened the door, she fell for him a smidgeon more.

"Apparently every tow truck in the county is out on a call," he explained as he dropped behind the wheel and pulled the door closed against the gusting wind. "But I got hold of Jonas. He's got a spare in his rig he'll bring right over. He's on his way now. So we'll be a few minutes late, but not out of the ballpark. They'll hold our reservation. I called."

Oh, and it was impossible not to fall even harder for a man who was so organized. "You just think of everything."

"So far, so good." Headlights cut through the rear window as a pickup pulled onto the shoulder behind them. That would be Jonas to the rescue. "Sit tight, and we'll be on the road before they can give our reservation away."

"That would be a real disaster," Katherine teased. "After going through all this for no food."

That made him laugh, the deep rumbling

sound she loved so much. For a moment their gazes met, and the impact rolled through her like joy. She felt his smile in her heart before he hopped back into the cold hail and angry wind and shut the door, leaving her with adoration filling her soul.

Did he dare to hope that this was all the disaster he was going to have to face for the evening? Even though he was soaking wet from the storm, Jack felt cautiously confident as he drove the last quarter mile. The road crested, and there was the restaurant, tucked in a corner of a small mall up ahead. Bright lights of the steakhouse glittered on the wet pavement, now that the precipitation had stopped.

"Wow, they're really busy," Katherine commented as he pulled into the mall.

He eased into place behind a long line of taillights glowing in the dark. He counted ten cars lined up ahead of him waiting to get into the restaurant's parking lot. He checked his watch. It was ten minutes after seven. Now he was glad he'd called the hostess. She'd promised to hold their table. Now, the challenge was to find parking in the jammed lot.

Luck was with him when a car backed out of

a spot, and he cut down the back row to slide into the vacated spot. Mission complete. After he'd helped Katherine from her seat, he tucked her hand in his, and it felt good. It felt right, with her at his side.

"Everyone in Bozeman must be here," Katherine said. "Look at the crowd."

"It's a good thing they're holding our reservation." Or they would be out of luck, he thought, studying the shivering couples standing beneath the awning, apparently willing to put up with the temperatures to wait for a table.

This place really must be good, he thought, eyeing the jammed vestibule. The waiting area was standing room only. He made eye contact with the woman behind the hostess's stand but she ignored him, grabbed a menu and sauntered out of sight. She wore an apron, clearly a waitress and not the hostess he'd talked to.

When he saw a man settle in behind the stand, a bad feeling hit him head-on. He felt Katherine's hand squeeze his, smelled the soft sweetness of her shampoo as she nudged close. "That's the guy I told you about."

What happened to the hostess? Jack planted his feet, determined to ward off the sense of doom settling over him like a thunder cell.

The man behind the stand smiled wide. "Caroline! It's good to see you again. Do you have a reservation?"

"Hi, Alvin. It's nice to see you, too." Katherine answered, polite as always. "I believe we do have a reservation. The name is Jack Munroe." She caught Jack's eye for confirmation.

His chest cinched so tight with powerful affection for her, he couldn't speak. He managed a nod, seeing nothing but her, and the seconds stretched into forever. It was a scary thing, how hard and fast he'd fallen in love with her.

He hadn't minded changing both tires in the storm; he didn't feel cold although he was wet to the skin. Usually, something like two flat tires in a hailstorm would rank on his worst-date-disaster list, but how could anything be bad when he was with Katherine? She smiled, and his soul brightened.

He didn't care what he had to take on. Any hardship would be easy as long as he was with her.

Alvin's voice broke into Jack's thoughts. "I'm sorry, Mr. Munroe, but we had to give your reservation away. We have a two-hour wait, and you're late."

Okay, Jack thought, hopes sinking. *This* is a

disaster of humungous proportion. A full ten on the Richter scale. A category-five hurricane.

He had a lot on the line. How in heaven's name was he going to be able to salvage this?

Chapter Twelve

Why wasn't she surprised? Katherine watched the hostess give Alvin a headshake and a "this is typical" sigh.

"You *never* listen," the hostess said. "I told you to hold the table."

"It's too bad. They were late anyway." Alvin pulled rank. "Caroline, would you like me to add you and your date to the waiting list?"

Katherine glanced around her at the crush of people. More hungry customers had arrived and were standing behind her and Jack. She heard a woman directly behind her whisper to her husband, "What? Did he say a two-hour wait? No sense getting on the waiting list. Let's get out of here."

Sounded like a good idea to her. She caught Jack's gaze and without words she knew what he was thinking. He crooked one brow. She nodded. "We won't get seated until nine. It's too long of a time to wait."

His hand tightened gently around hers; it was like a connection of the spirit. "There's another restaurant at the other end of the mall—"

"It has a ninety-minute wait," a man said, standing to Jack's left. "The wife and I thought, forget that, and came over here, and look what that got us. But by the time we drive back over to the other place and wait, it'll be nine o'clock either way."

"Thanks." Jack turned to Katherine. "What do you want to do?"

He made it sound as if anything she said would be okay. Like they were in this together. "At this point, I'd be happy with fast food from a drive-through that we eat in the car."

Jack leaned closer. "Why don't we see if we can order here to go? Eat in the car? It might not take that long, and we'd get a good steak out of the deal."

"I vote yes."

"Then let me grab some menus, Caroline." He moved away from her, leaving her laughing.

She liked him. Way too much. She knew she was watching him with her heart, seeing not with just her eyes, as he exchanged some words with Alvin, who didn't look too happy but handed over two menus.

As she studied her menu, practically crushed against Jack's chest in the crowded waiting area, she hardly noticed the words before her. All she could see was Jack. See there were new layers to him she never would have guessed existed on the first night they'd met. He was resourceful and solved problems sensibly. Even standing in a fine restaurant wet and wind-blown, he still had a sense of humor.

"I've got my mind made up," he said, snapping his menu closed.

"Me, too." She wasn't referring to the menu choices, but the man towering over her.

When the hostess was ready, they gave their orders. Jack ordered a couple of appetizers so they could have immediate sustenance. Katherine followed Jack's lead through the waiting room, the jammed vestibule and onto the sidewalk. The storm clouds tore apart to reveal a half moon shimmering like platinum, lighting their way back to the SUV.

"This wasn't what I had in mind for our first date." Jack apologized as his hand came to rest between her shoulder blades, not exactly hugging her as much as a gentle pressure guiding her. It felt protective and nice.

She definitely felt safe with Jack. "This isn't what I envisioned either, but it could be worse."

"We both know that from experience. I don't want to end up like Alvin. Get turned down for a second date and then wind up on your worst dating list."

"The jury's still out." She couldn't help teasing him. "We'll see what other disasters are lurking in the next few hours before I decide if you merit a place on my list. You never know, maybe it's smooth sailing ahead."

"I like your optimism, Caroline."

He paused to open the back passenger door, his hand a branding presence on her upper back. She looked down, afraid her feelings were on her face. What if he could see through her too easily? She accepted a hand up onto the back seat.

"I'll be right back with those appetizers," he promised, handing her the keys.

"You must really trust me to give me these. I *could* drive away."

"I know where you live." He winked, pressed the door shut and ambled away with that confident, athletic stride of his.

She watched him go, feeling the sigh rising up from the bottom of her soul. I'm in so much trouble. I'm falling in love with him.

Definitely the uh-oh stage.

* * *

Jack knifed a bite of filet and considered the evening so far. Did the pluses outweigh the minuses? He probably wouldn't find out until after dessert. "There's a bonus to eating in the car. It'll be harder for you to duck out on me."

"It will depend on what you have for dessert, whether I run or stay." She balanced the plate on her lap, neat as a pin, daintily slicing a tiny bite off her steak.

"You're a good sport, Katherine. I'm trying to think of any other woman I've dated who wouldn't have turned on me after losing the dinner reservation."

"Turning on you would have made no sense. I was starving." The glitter in her eyes, one of humor and *maybe* something deeper, said otherwise.

That was exactly what he wanted to know. "This steak is the best I've ever had. It was worth all it took to get here. Even—" Rain drops began to ping on the roof. "—this ambiance. It's one of a kind."

"It's memorable. Hey, I haven't asked you how Hayden liked working with Marin. Am I right in thinking that today was her last volunteer day?"

Jack nodded, chewing, considering how to

answer that tactfully, but he told the truth. "She hasn't been happy about this, or a lot of the changes I've imposed on her. I'm not sure how this will work out, or if I'm doing the right thing by standing firm or if I'm pushing too hard. I just have to hang in there and have faith that good intentions matter in the long run."

"I know they do."

"I've thought about what you said. About your dad. That his staying and his leadership made a bigger impact than your mom's leaving. That's what I want to show my daughter. The loss of her mother is always going to be a wound she carries, but you also said something else I think is true. That we learn to live again, even with the scar."

"We have my dad to thank for that. It's his wisdom. And my grandmother's. You credit me with far too much."

Modest. He loved that about her; he couldn't quite believe she didn't know how remarkable she was. When she opened herself up like this, it was easy to see the shadows she carried. Everyone had them, but not everyone coped as well.

Heaven knew he hadn't coped well. "I see a lot of difficult things in my line of work. Accidents. Violence. Kidnappings. A lot of injustice. I always wondered how good people dealt with the consequences of those things. Did it ruin their lives? Sometimes, I saw that it did. But I didn't know until it happened to me what it took to get past the trauma."

She stopped eating to watch him. The overhead dome light glowed enough to see the secrets shadowing her eyes and in the air between them.

"Several years ago, a hot July afternoon, the last seventeen minutes of my shift, I was responding to a call," he found himself saying. "A multiple-car injury accident, blocking a major route north of the city. Heidi, Hayden and I, we had plans to go out for hamburgers and a movie. That's what was on my mind, not wanting to disappoint them if I was late."

He closed his eyes against the images. "When I pulled up, I saw a minivan just like ours. Medium blue, same make and model, sideswiped at high speed by an industrial van. Both vehicles were destroyed and blocking the intersection. It was a mess. Another unit had pulled in ahead of me. Decker held up a hand, told me to stay back. That I didn't want to see this."

It was his wife. Katherine heard that thought as if it were her own, in her mind and in her heart. She felt the cold wall of grief. Of Jack's grief. She reached across the plates on the seat between them and laid her hand on the back of his.

"There was nothing I could do. Nothing anyone could do. She was already gone. It was impossible to accept. What was harder was learning she'd caused the accident on the way to pick up Hayden at school. She'd run a red light. The impact of the collision had involved other cars. Two kids and their mother were hurt. They all recovered eventually." He fell silent.

The air seemed to vibrate with his pain. "This had to be devastating for you and Hayden. It was sudden."

"Wait, what am I doing? This is too much information. I didn't mean to talk about this tonight. I've blown it. You're waiting for the dessert so you can get home."

How could she feel so connected emotionally to this man that she could feel his pain, and yet he couldn't sense her feelings? "I'm not reaching for my cell to call a cab."

"For all I know you have a cab company on speed dial."

"I'll be able to hold off dialing for a while." Humor softened the gentle curves of her face.

The compassion he felt made it easier to let go of his worries. Maybe the success of a first date wasn't so much that every thing and every conversation had to go right. Perhaps what really mattered was the emotional connection forged between two people.

Maybe that's what Katherine was looking for, too. Maybe this evening wouldn't be as bust as he thought. The sight of her slim hand resting over his, soft and small and delicate, broke him open in a way he'd never experienced before.

"When the lab reports came back with Heidi's toxicology report, I was stunned." He paused. "I didn't believe it. Not even after I saw her credit card statement detailing that she'd been at a local bar, and it wasn't the first time. She handled the finances so I didn't suspect. I also found cancelled checks to liquor stores."

"She hid that from you."

"She did. It was against her beliefs, and she hid it from me. Looking back, I should have known. Heidi had several miscarriages after Hayden. The doctor finally told her no more. I think her grief was something I just couldn't help her with. I tried."

"But she kept that from you, too."

"I don't want to lose Hayden the same way."

"Is that why you moved here?"

He nodded. "The stages of grief sound clichéd until you go through them, or watch someone you love move through them. Hayden hit depression and seemed to stick there. She started being unreliable. She lost all of her close friends. Made new friendships with kids who got into trouble and drank."

"I bet that scared you."

"At the first sign of it, I gave a knee-jerk reaction. I had to protect her. She's still my little girl. I called some of my old friends who lived in other states, looking to relocate. I figured it might be better to start over somewhere without all the memories."

"After my mom left, the memories were the hardest part." She thought of her teen years and had to push down those recollections. "Maybe sad memories are always the toughest."

"I think you can try to deny them or block them. But they stick with you, whether you want to acknowledge them or not." He grimaced. "Too much information, right?"

"No."

"I'm not going to top Alvin on your date-disaster list?"

Like an arrow to her heart. Katherine closed her eyes. Of course he didn't know what he'd said. "You're not going to have to worry about topping my *funniest* date disaster list. Alvin isn't dethroned yet."

He looked at her for a moment, as if he could see past her calm and her will, her struggle to keep the past buried. Panic jolted through her like a lightning strike. Had she said too much? What if he'd heard what she hadn't said? Dani's words rang through Katherine's mind. *If this Jack guy isn't the kind of man to accept what happened to you, then he isn't good enough for you.*

Just be rational, Katherine. She knew Danielle was right. It was what she believed, too. But a woman's heart didn't run on logic. She cared about Jack, she was falling for Jack. And she didn't know enough about him to be sure he would understand. She suspected he might. She hoped he might.

But if he didn't, his rejection was going to hurt. Once, it hadn't occurred to her that a man might not understand. Until Kevin, a man she'd known all her life, a man she'd come to love with all her heart, didn't want her after he knew the truth. His words still haunted her. *You've ruined the most sacred gifts a wife can give to her husband. If a woman can't keep herself for marriage for any reason, then she's not a good Christian.*

For any reason. As if she hadn't fought as hard as she could. As if she'd chosen what had happened to her. Kevin's love had vanished, just like that. When she most needed his acceptance, he'd looked at her with contempt.

One man's lack of compassion is not what I want to determine my life, she thought, willing down the panic. One man's heart wasn't big enough to be compassionate. It didn't mean another man's wouldn't be. That Jack's wouldn't be.

"Katherine, look at that."

Jack's baritone shattered her thoughts, and she followed his gesture toward the side window where an elderly couple, walking hand in hand, approached the neighboring car. The low murmur of their voices, the close intimacy of it, spoke of a devoted, successful marriage.

See, it wasn't a dream. It happened to some people. It could happen to her. Katherine watched the husband unlock and hold the door for his wife. Although rain slicked the side window, she didn't miss the honest affection the man and woman exchanged with a simple look, in a single moment in time.

There was real love, the kind that lasted. It made her wish. Just wish.

"If you're done," Jack said, "I'll take this

stuff back to the hostess. It was nice of her to trust us with their real plates instead of plastic. It made this a little nicer."

"Plus, it's easier to cut the steak with a real knife instead of a plastic one." Katherine managed a smile. Managed to tuck away her wishes and dreams and the vestiges of the past. "What about dessert?"

"I figure we can eat it at your place, if that's okay. I'm stuffed." With a grin he began stacking the plates and forks and setting them into the sturdy take-out bag they'd gotten from the hostess.

The neighboring car backed out of its space and out of sight, and Jack slung open the door. "I'll be back."

"I may be waiting. I may not be," she teased to make him smile. She should be happy, but disappointment was filling her up. She didn't know why.

"At least we didn't get any flat tires on the way back." Jack pulled to a stop in a space marked Guest Parking. "How about that dessert?"

"Come in. I'll make tea."

A good sign. She seemed relaxed and happy and glad about how things were going.

He was, too. He'd seen the look on her face when she'd watched the elderly couple getting into their car. They both wanted the same thing. Good to know.

Not that he could relax, because the evening wasn't over. There was still time for a disaster or two, but so far so good. He also had Hayden to win over and that wasn't going to be easy.

Give it time, he thought, hurrying around to open the passenger door and take her hand. He was rewarded with a demure smile, pure sweetness. If this didn't work out, he was going to be a mess. He was going to get hurt something bad.

Don't think about that, Jack. Just take it one step at a time. Right now, this step was pretty nice. He grabbed the bagged desserts from the floor, closed the door and locked the vehicle.

"Oh, no. My living-room lights are on." She froze in her tracks in the middle of the wet, slick parking lot. "It's probably the twins. Maybe you want to rethink our dessert plans."

"I can handle your sisters."

"You haven't met the twins. They might send you running."

"I'm tough. I can take it."

"Okay, but don't say I didn't warn you."

The wind battered at the ends of her hair, brushing against the soft angle of her jaw. A lock tumbled into her eyes and he swept it back behind her ear.

Tender feelings rendered him helpless. Nothing could stop him from falling all the way, irrevocably, in love with her.

Chapter Thirteen

The instant the front door closed behind Jack, Aubrey poked her head in from clearing the dining-room table. "I like him."

"Totally." Ava paused with a stack of dessert plates in hand. "He's more dreamy than I thought."

"He's so into you, Kath." Aubrey vibrated with happiness as she went back to the table and scooped up the good china teacups with care. "It's so wow."

"Super wow," Ava corrected from the kitchen.

Katherine leaned her forehead against the cool plane of the door. How she'd survived the stress of the twins and the end of her date with Jack was too much to contemplate right now. She only knew that she'd survived intact.

Well, almost intact. It was surprising how fast a wish could go from tiny to full-blown. As she dragged herself away from the door, she caught sight of Jack's truck through the window, taillights glowing in the shimmering dark as he drove out of the complex.

"So?" Aubrey looked up from stacking the plates in the dishwasher's bottom basket.

Ava plopped the cups on the counter. "What do you think?"

"It went really well tonight." Katherine grabbed a dishcloth from the top drawer. "Wonderfully well."

"You sound very happy." Ava leaned close. "Tell us. It was a really good date, right?"

Aubrey dragged out the top rack with a clank. "Don't you see? She's in the uh-oh phase."

"Hey, stop analyzing me. We can discuss the reason why neither of you are dating." Katherine ran the cloth under the tap and added a couple drops of dishwashing soap. "Ava, what happened to that chef guy you were serious about?"

"Three dates. That doesn't qualify as serious. Stop trying to change the subject."

"Those white roses have to be from Jack. Not that she'll admit it," Aubrey said conspiratorially to her twin.

"He's serious."

"I'm not listening." Katherine left the room, heading for the table with a few crumbs on it. She scrubbed until the wood gleamed.

Yeah, she thought Jack was serious, too. It had felt *right* when she'd been beside him, with her hand tucked in his much bigger one. She'd never felt so safe and comfortable simply from holding a man's hand. That had to be a sign, right?

It was another sign that she'd never had so many things not go as planned on a first date and still have it turn out fine. He'd made her laugh. He'd solved every problem that came his way with a sensible competence she found highly attractive.

"Are you going to kick us out?" Ava asked from the sink. "Or are you going to let us hang?"

"C'mon, let us hang with you," Aubrey pleaded as she shut the dishwasher up tight. "We came just in case things didn't go well and you didn't want to be alone. We can go, but we don't have anything else to do."

"I was just going to read. You might as well stay."

"Thanks, Kath," they said in unison, turning back to wiping down their halves of the counter.

She loved her sisters. Without words, they understood how important this date had been to her. "I'm going to go change."

"Not too much," Ava began.

"We like you just the way you are," Aubrey said.

Katherine rolled her eyes. Sisters. Blessings she thanked God for every day. What if the evening had been a disappointment? *Then* she would really have needed their company.

She peeled off her date clothes and sank into comfy fleece sweats. As she was shoving her feet into a pair of thick wool socks, it hit her. When Jack had talked about the loss of his wife and of her problems, he didn't sound judgmental of her. Or angry or disapproving. Because he had loved her.

Maybe that was a sign of a man with a heart big enough.

Maybe. She would pray on it. Then she'd have to wait and see. See if he called. See if he was still interested after the tire thing and eating dinner in the car and then putting up with her sisters. Face it, Katherine, he might have taken that as a sign to run. Or, at the very least, he could be suffering from dater's remorse.

Please, the deepest part of her heart pleaded,

let this work. Let him be the one. She felt totally vulnerable, as if tonight's closeness to Jack had peeled back every defense layer, leaving her spirit exposed, like the root of a rose when the dirt was brushed away.

A sign that she was now in the point-of-no-return phase. She was falling so hard for this man, if he didn't understand, if he turned away from her, she might never be the same.

After locking the door after Mrs. Garcia, Jack couldn't figure out what was bugging him. The date had been great. What had gone right had far outweighed what had gone wrong. He ought to be grinning ear to ear. He'd even enjoyed dessert at Katherine's place with her younger twin sisters, who were as funny as could be.

Tonight, he'd gotten a good glimpse of the woman Katherine was, confirming that the surface calm and kindness went deep. That she valued family and marriage. He'd learned they were surprisingly compatible in the ways they handled problems, enjoyed each other's sense of humor and rolled with the punches when things didn't go as planned. They were on the same page on a lot of things like values and living a faith-centered life and wanting a serious relationship. They both liked steaks and chocolate fudge cake.

It was a good start. Tonight, being with her had felt like a fit, a perfect match. As if heaven was saying, see, this is the one who fits in your life.

And, Jack knew, in his heart.

He grabbed the remote from the coffee table and clicked on the TV, keeping the volume low so it wouldn't wake Hayden. He found a news show and left it on for noise. He felt restless. Troubled. He couldn't put his finger on it.

Maybe his Bible would help. He reached for the well-worn leather volume on the middle shelf of the six-foot bookcase. That's when he noticed the shelf below, haphazard and untidy, certainly not the way Mrs. Garcia had left it when she'd done the cleaning. Looking at the thick, tall photo albums made the dam break, and all his personal troubles flooded to the surface, powerful enough to rock him.

I shouldn't have talked about Heidi tonight. His hand seemed to move of its own volition, withdrawing one of the albums and opening it to the middle page. Heidi had gone through a scrapbooking phase and her artistic talent had made the simple pages into beauty.

Our Summer Vacation was the title, in flowing silver letters with all kinds of color and framework and style. The past flooded him as he studied the pictures they'd taken of the three of them huddled around a Welcome to Yellowstone sign. Hayden so young, she had to be around nine, her hair drawn back by a pink headband, her innocence and happiness shining as bright as the sun. Heidi's eyes were hidden behind dark glasses, and her smile was forced. It had been a hard trip for her. She'd never come back fully after realizing she would never have more children.

Sometimes, as much as you tried, as much as you loved someone, it wasn't enough. He'd seen too much in his work and he knew, good people had problems. They were all flawed. Life happened, and he'd done everything right, never put his work or himself above his family and his faith.

He'd done it all in the right way, and still he'd lost his wife. Now he feared he could lose his daughter in a fundamental or spiritual way. He wished he could go back in time so he would know not to take Heidi's reassurances that she was fine for the truth. But it was impossible. All he could do now was to forgive her for the wrong choices she'd made out of pain. He closed the book with a thud that echoed in the room. It felt so empty, despite the drone of the television and his little girl upstairs.

He didn't know if he'd thought to forgive Heidi before this. The last few years had been tough: grieving, parenting Hayden alone, trying to make the right choices and the right decisions. Life had a way of carrying you forward whether you meant to or not.

He returned the album to the shelf.

"Dad?" Wrapped in her housecoat Hayden padded silently into the room. "You were looking at the albums."

She sounded confrontational; he knew a lot hid beneath the surface. "Yep."

"You probably forgot what Mom looked like, huh? Must have come as a real shock."

"I miss your mother every day. I suspect I always will miss the chance to make the past right."

Hayden shrugged, retreating into sarcasm. Her chin came up, her eyes filled with pain. "It's like, yay, she's gone, so I'll just date, right? Whatever."

"I believe it's what your mother would want."

"She'd *want* to be replaced? Forgotten? Yeah, right."

This was the problem, Jack thought. When

he'd had that long counseling session with Marin, this is what she'd said to look for. It was easy to get stuck somewhere on the grieving process. The important thing was to help Hayden move along in her grief and to accept, finally. So she could move past this broken place in her life.

That was what he was trying to do. "No one can replace your mom, Hayden."

"You seem to think Katherine McKaslin can. You were out with her, right? I'm not a dumb kid anymore."

"You're the smartest kid I know. And you're going to grow up to be intelligent, good and kind, just like your mom."

Tears flooded Hayden's eyes. She whipped away to hide them.

"You're so like her, Hayden." Maybe this was why he had such a hard time seeing Hayden as a teenager, seeing her as a young lady. Because he saw so much of Heidi in her. "Losing your mom nearly killed me, you know that. I haven't liked going on living without her, but it's what we have to do."

Hayden sniffed. "I'm not gonna forget her. I won't do it. I can't just say, fine, I loved you and stuff but now you're not here so, too bad. I'll just have a great time. Yippee."

"Oh, baby." He'd never quite seen the problem or the solution so clearly. For all his good intentions over the past few years, for all his love and his devotion to his daughter, he'd needed help with this. Marin's help. Katherine's influence. God's guidance. But he had it figured out now, he really did. "I'm not dating Katherine to replace your mom. I would never want that."

Still faced away from him, her shoulders hunched, his daughter was utter misery. She shook with silent sobs.

"But you don't have to stay miserable to hold onto your mom. I think that's what I've done too, let that sadness simmer into bitterness because as long as I keep grieving her, I think she won't be forgotten. But that's not true."

Harder sobs.

"Katherine is a nice lady, and I like her. I'm going to date her, but not because I've forgotten your mom. Because I want to honor her. She impacted my life in so many positive ways. That's what we should take with us. All the good things. We should hold those memories close and keep on living. She wants us to have good lives."

"Wants us? She doesn't want anything, Dad. She's g-gone."

He placed his hand on her shoulder, a father's tender love filling him. He wanted to protect her from this pain, to stop her tears, to obliterate her misery, but she couldn't walk through it to the other side if he did. "Your mom isn't here anymore, it's true, but she's alive in heaven."

"You c-can pray, but it doesn't bring her b-back."

"Her spirit is alive and that means her love for you is alive. Don't stop loving her. Do you think she wants that?"

Hayden shook her head.

"Love her the right way, in prayer. Make good choices in your life to honor her. She's not here like she was, but your mom's love for you is forever. Not even death can stop that."

She hung her head, as if even more miserable.

Words were words, he knew, until you felt them, until you believed them soul-deep. He reached for the photo albums again. "You were looking at these tonight?"

A watery nod, as if she were hurting too much to speak.

He knew just how that felt. "Do you remember our trip to Yellowstone? The first thing we did was look for buffalo, remember?"

A single nod.

He sensed Hayden looking against her will. He flipped open to the page so she could see. "A bull stepped right out in the road in front of us. And while he stood there for twenty-one minutes, we got a real close view. Remember how hairy he was?"

"Mom was afraid of him, like he was going to gore us, so you took us to a restaurant and ordered buffalo burgers for all of us." Hayden almost smiled, then her face collapsed and she fell silent, tears on her face.

"It's okay to laugh. It *was* funny. Remember how your mom felt much better after lunch? She wasn't scared anymore."

She crossed her arms around her middle, as if holding the pain inside. "Don't."

"I know it hurts, but it will get better. Then, when you look at these pictures you'll remember the good things. The love. The happiness. That's what we get to keep."

Her gaze traveled to the photos, bright on the open pages, frozen in time. It was hard to know what she was thinking. She snapped the books shut and took them with her as she ambled toward the stairs.

It was late, and she looked tired. Jack knew she'd had a long day. "I'm proud that you stuck it out at the shelter. I know you didn't like it.

Marin told me you were doing a great job. She was impressed with you."

"I just wanted to get the work over and done with." Hayden hugged the albums to her as paused. "Dad?"

"Yeah?"

"I get what you're trying to say. I just…" She shrugged again, his little girl, clutching the photo albums full of so many memories, books made with everlasting love, looking both so young and so grown-up in the same moment. "G'night."

"Good night. Don't forget to say your prayers."

"Yeah." Wistful. A little confused. And she was gone.

It wasn't easy to let go of grieving, he knew. Sometimes grief was the only way to hold on to a loved one who had passed. Hayden was a smart, good girl. She was going to get through this. He'd make sure of it.

The past and those we've loved would always be a part of us, he thought, in this room with a few pictures and photo albums of the past. But it was the future that gave him hope now. A future where his daughter was happy and growing up and living a good, quality life.

As for his future, that had been a huge

question mark for many years. Until now. Whatever steps he chose had to be good for Hayden; there was no question about that. Maybe the trials he'd been through, and those numerous first dates that had never worked out, had happened for a reason. To bring him here. To Katherine. To perfect Katherine.

He turned to the Bible he still held, weighing it in his hands. Comforting. Sure. Eminently thankful, he bowed his head, grateful for his blessings.

Katherine woke up, the scream dying in her throat. The sounds of her panicked breathing a ghostly echo in the room. The nightmare shredded into a thousand pieces and disappeared as she flicked on the bedside-table lamp. The sudden light felt too bright. Her eyes hurt as it spilled over the tabletop and her Bible, chasing back the darkness.

She dragged herself into a sitting position and her arms felt weak. Her hands shook hard as she grabbed the covers and shoved them away. She felt nauseated, sick. Wet with sweat. The taste of fear lingered in her mouth. Emptiness had hollowed out her soul, just the way it had over fifteen years ago.

Everyone has wounds in their lives. It's not

so much that you erase that wound from your heart, as much as you learn to move past the pain. To live and learn to trust others even with that old wound. Why did her words come back to her, the ones she'd said to Jack a while ago?

Maybe because tonight she'd reopened the wrong that nothing could make right. Making light of first-date disasters as if the only kind of dating disaster would be funny, and not dangerous. Worrying about what Jack would think if he knew she'd been date-raped as a college freshman. What he would think of the nine months following that…oh, that was a time she could not bear to allow into her consciousness.

The simple act of remembering tore through her soul.

All the years of counseling, of help and understanding from her family and pastor had helped her learn to cope and heal enough to live her life. But the emotional wound would never go away. It haunted her on nights like this. She'd given this up to God, but it still haunted her. It still felt like a brand on her spirit. Kevin had rejected her because of it.

Would Jack?

In the wee hours of the night, when the dark was so suffocating and powerful, it dimmed the brightness of their emotional connection and of the good, positive experience of simply having dinner with him.

The darkness made the shadows inside her deeper and harder to see past.

Chapter Fourteen

The shadows from the nightmare seemed to stick in the light of day. Church service had helped, and having lunch with her sisters and brother had, too. But now that she was back home, alone with the silence of the house surrounding her, she noticed the shadows again, lurking just below the surface.

Maybe some noise would help. She slipped a CD in the player, hit Play and hoped that the "Moonlight Sonata" would ease some of her anxiety. She plopped on the couch, put her feet on the coffee table and picked up her book. Even with the soothing music, she couldn't concentrate.

The phone rang. What were the odds that was one of her sisters? Ava had called twice, Aubrey once. Danielle had called. Stepsister

Rebecca, who'd been out of the loop being busy with college, had called, all wanting the scoop.

In the last two hours Katherine had dodged so many questions about Jack, she didn't know if she had enough energy to do it one more time. At least, not without fortifying herself with chocolate first.

She found enough oomph to check the extension, but the ID screen said it was Jack. Her hand was reaching to answer the phone before her mind had made the conscious decision. "I hope this means you made it home last night without disaster on those spare tires."

"Roger that. I'm not calling at a bad time, right?"

"Right. I'm just trying to read a book."

"Trying?"

"My phone keeps ringing. My sisters, mostly."

"Your sisters are a big part of your life."

"I would disown them, but then who would look after them? What can I say, they need me." Since she was up, she wandered into the kitchen. Surely she had some chocolate somewhere. "Why are you calling?"

"I wanted to make sure you weren't starting to think over last night and getting dater's remorse."

"We've both been there before. Fortunately I've had the syndrome often so I recognize the symptoms, and I haven't noticed any so far."

"That's good."

"Of course, it's early yet. We'll see how this call turns out."

"Sure, add to the pressure."

"How about you?" She tugged open the pantry door. "Are you experiencing any signs of dating remorse?"

"Only that I spilled my personal stuff and you didn't. You stayed mysteriously silent."

"Probably because I was eating."

"Notice how that didn't stop *me?*"

This man made her laugh. The more she wanted him, the more real it was that she would have to tell him about… Don't think about it yet, Katherine. She scanned the pantry—the only chocolate she spied was a package of baking chips. "I like that you think I'm mysteriously silent. I think that's how we'll keep it."

"And I'm trying to politely pry into your story."

Right here was a good place to tell him about that stubborn but devout seventeen-year-old girl who'd graduated a year early from the local high school and insisted on going away to college. Away from the protective arms of her dad and stepmother, away from the safety net of her siblings and childhood friends. Away from everything she knew. Not understanding that the world wasn't as safe as the one she'd grown up in.

Now wasn't the time to tell him about that, not on the phone.

"Sorry. No prying allowed, mister. I'm mysteriously silent, remember?"

"Mysteriously silent and impervious to interrogation techniques?"

"Absolutely." Wise in the ways of plastic packaging, she didn't even try to rip the bag open. She went to the top drawer and plucked a pair of scissors out of the drawer organizer. "I didn't see you at the early service this morning. I'm assuming you made the later one?"

"Yep. Hayden and I had some issues to discuss. We made it to the last service just as they were starting the opening prayer." His baritone dipped, serious.

She could feel the weight of it like a hundred-pound barbell on her chest. Here it comes, she thought as she snipped the corner off the bag. The first real obstacle—Hayden. "How is she doing?"

"Better, I think. It's hard to tell because the

male brain cannot wrap around the workings of the female mind. She says she's fine and I know she's not, but I think she means she's doing better than she has been. Our talk started after I got home last night and we picked it up this morning."

The truth was, she cared about Hayden. She popped a few chips into her mouth. She braced herself for him to say this wasn't going to be good for Hayden. "How does she feel about our date? The last thing I want to do is cause her more problems."

"You're not. My daughter has some grief issues she's dealing with. They're going to be with her for some time to come. With your mom leaving when you were young, I know you understand. I have to do what's best for my little girl, hands down."

"I already know that about you. That's what I want, too."

"I've known that from the start." His words were warm, his baritone inviting her to relax, to let down her guard, to open up.

And there it was, this intense emotional closeness to him. A connection that could erase the miles separating them and breach the walls of her condo and dig like a fishhook into her spirit, binding her to him.

This is way too fast, she thought as she plopped onto the couch cushion. They'd been on one date. She could make a two-page list of all the things she didn't know about him. And probably a five-line list of all the things she did.

This wasn't sensible, falling so fast and hard like this. She'd passed the fail-safe point, and if this didn't work out, she knew there wasn't a safe way back. How did she put on the brakes? How did she slow down her feelings? He was like gravity pulling her soul to his and it wasn't practical or sensible or orderly, but frightening and uncertain. She had no way to predict doom or safety.

And that was how she'd been able to come back after the rape and its consequences. Safe, practical, sensible, predictable. She'd built her life on that, and she had thrived. Like anyone, she had her good days and her harder ones, but everyone had pain in their lives. She had her faith to help her. And, she knew, it would help her now. Strengthen her to face whatever came of this.

"Hayden has her skiing lesson this week, so I have a question. How about you meet me up at the lodge?"

"Are you going to try to ski?"

"Not down the advanced runs."

His words were warm with humor and curled around her heart like the coziness from a wood fire. Oh, she was so in love with this man. There was no way to stop it. No way to hold back such a powerful emotional force. So she took a deep breath and sealed her fate. "I'll see you there."

Her fateful words haunted her into the next day. Katherine zipped her coat as she stepped out into the crisp, blustery day, trying to ignore Marin's and Holly's question. The one she'd been asked at least six hundred times today.

"I'm seeing him tomorrow," she told them as they wove their way around the parked cars. "And before you ask another question, no, it's not an official date, we're just getting together for skiing and dinner after or something."

"Sure, he calls you up the day *after* your first date. Obviously he's *hardly* interested," Holly agreed, trawling for her keys in her enormous tote. "I mean, how indifferent can a guy get?"

"Exactly." Marin led the way to Holly's car. "I mean, how many guys call right away? They say they will, and they do. I think it's fairly common."

"Enough!" Katherine rolled her eyes. How much did she have to put up with? She knew her friends cared. She knew all the calls from her sisters were because they were rooting for her happiness. But a girl could only take so much. "I'm officially out of the hesitant stage, so you can stop now."

Holly beeped the car doors unlocked with her remote. "Are you serious? You're ready to admit you like him?"

"The uh-oh stage," Marin said. "I named that stage. It's where the doom of romance really starts. When you start caring. *That's* when they've got you."

"I feel so much better now," Katherine commented as she climbed into the back seat. "What if I told you it's more serious than that?"

"The point-of-no-return phase," Marin said. "Although I call it the doom phase."

Holly climbed behind the wheel and started the car. "You're not helping, Marin."

"Sorry. Too many years of marital counseling jades you just a tad. So, Katherine, you must feel pretty serious about this man."

Serious. Why did her stomach knot up as if she were facing a jail sentence? "I haven't had a connection like this with anyone before. I don't know what it is. It's very…encompassing. Intense. It's like he just reached in and grabbed hold of my heart."

"That's seriously serious." Marin flipped around in her seat. "Are you ready for this?"

"Can anyone be?" Katherine held up her hands, feeling helpless. She couldn't think of a single word to describe how she felt. "I've never felt so strongly before, not even for Kevin, and I was in love with him. It scares me."

"That's how it is when love is real." Holly backed the car out of the parking spot. "It's scary because you have to trust that person so much with your heart and who you are. It's like you have to open the most private rooms in your heart and let him in. That is one of the hardest things, to be honest and love without defense. After you've been hurt like you have, Katherine, it's natural to try hard to keep him out of those places. But real love can never work that way. You have to let him in, just as he has to let you in."

Marin nodded in agreement. "Are you going to trust Jack enough to open up to him the way you did with Kevin? Or not?"

"It wouldn't have mattered if I had told Kevin before he asked me to marry him. He still would have had the same reaction." She closed her eyes, unwilling to see Jack reacting the same way. Unable to let herself even imagine such a negative response. It would do more than hurt her, it would devastate her. "I made mistakes with Kevin."

Mostly in keeping him at an emotional distance. Marin and Holly were right. She'd never trusted Kevin enough to let him in close. For some inexplicable reason, Jack could do that by the simple force of his personality or some heaven-sent design; she didn't know which. She only knew that Jack had gotten beneath her defenses. Every single one of them.

As Holly drove the few blocks to the bookstore, their conversation turned to other things. But Katherine felt stuck in place, as if the back of her mind was working out what her friends had been trying to tell her. What she had been trying to figure out for herself.

When they pulled into the parking lot, she felt her spirit brighten, the way it did when she was near Jack. All it took was one glance to see his state cruiser nosed in at the sidewalk in a parking spot directly in front of the store.

If she was lucky, Marin wouldn't notice or comment. Katherine unbuckled her seat belt, prepared just in case Marin started up again. "Thanks for driving, Holly. Bye!"

The instant her feet touched pavement, Katherine whirled to close the door and caught sight of Jack through the front window, in his uniform. The light within her brightened. She wasn't aware of moving, but she was at the door, pulling it open with a jingle of the overhead bell. Jack turned toward the sound, looking over his shoulder. Their eyes met and Katherine felt the impact rock through her soul.

I love him. The realization blazed through her like a meteor. The sensible part of her seemed to fade away until there was only feeling. Only happiness. Only certainty.

"Katherine." He seemed to light up. "Your cousin has been telling me what a good catch you are."

"Too bad I have to fire her now." Katherine gave Kelly a death-ray glare, but her cousin and best employee seemed immune to its effects. "Are you on your way to work?"

"Dropping off Hayden first." He pocketed his wallet, took the plastic bag Kelly handed him over the counter and ambled her way. "You look beautiful."

She missed a step, staring up at him as if he'd started speaking Swahili. Then she recovered and smiled shyly up at him. "Thank you."

He had a thousand things he wanted to ask her about. All the things he didn't know and they hadn't shared. Not that he had time at this exact moment. And not that he wanted to get personal with so many members of her family watching. The twins had been changing the display tables in the front of the store and were obviously listening without any attempt to conceal it or even to appear as if they were working.

Kelly, who'd rung up his book purchase, was leaning expectantly over the counter, eyes bright and curious. Even the brother, Spence, whom he had yet to officially meet, had turned partway from his computer monitor and, while continuing to work, had cocked an ear toward his now-open door.

Not exactly a desirable courting atmosphere. Definitely not a private one. "Walk me to my ride?"

"Sure. Maybe then everyone can get back to work."

Ava and Aubrey didn't budge. Neither did Kelly.

Jack opened the door for Katherine. She brushed by him, close enough for him to smell the soft floral fragrance of her shampoo, to see the light gold of her hair gleam like platinum in the sunlight. She was so feminine and fragile; tenderness reared up inside him as he followed her outside. She made him feel ten feet tall.

As if nervous or unsure, she folded a lock of hair behind her ear. "I've been meaning to run something by you. It's about Hayden."

"Uh-oh." That can't be good. He tried to focus, but all he seemed to notice was the porcelain fineness of Katherine's complexion and the delicate cut of her jaw. A wave of affection rolled through him, filling him to the brim.

"No, it's not bad, so don't worry. It's that Hayden's volunteering here was your idea. I was willing to see how it went, but she surprised us. She's a hard worker."

"And her attitude?"

Katherine wisely skipped that one. "This will be her last week, and Spence and I are so pleased with her work ethic, that we'd like to pay her minimum wage for the hours she's worked."

"That's generous, but it would defeat the purpose."

"It's still something Spence and I would like to do. Even Ava said so. It's one thing to have a teenager work off a debt of sorts. It's another when she works harder than Ava."

He was in serious trouble. He couldn't say no to her. He was hands-down, one-hundred-percent, all the way in love with this woman. The kind of abiding love that did not end, that did not diminish, that gave a man purpose and hope.

"All right," he agreed. What else could he do? "It'll be a reward for working hard."

"Good justification." Katherine flashed a dazzling smile.

Yep, he'd do just about anything for her. Move mountains. Ensure happiness. Provide eternal devotion. "I've got to go. Mrs. Garcia will be picking Hayden up in a few hours. But I'll see you tomorrow afternoon?"

"Unless I change my mind." She took a step back, smiling up at him. "That's unlikely."

"Good to know." Jack's dimples cut deep into his cheeks as he stepped off the curb, a big bear of a man, outlined by the bright spring sunshine.

His gaze held hers a second longer, and for that instant in time she could see the future. Her dream for the future. Maybe his. She didn't know which. Only the long solid closeness of an intimate marriage, where they were best friends, partners, confidantes, best everything.

"My luck with second dates is much better," he said as he opened his car door. "You wait and see."

Katherine didn't know if it was a promise or a threat. It felt like both. Maybe Marin was right in calling it the doom phase because she was hooked, not just by the heart, but deeper. As if her spirit was linked to his irrevocably.

She squinted in the sun, watching Jack's cruiser cross the lot, whip out onto the street and disappear in traffic. She shivered in the crisp wind, feeling, just *feeling*. No defenses, no buffer, just pure hope.

"Katherine?"

She startled, surprised to realize Kelly was standing beside her.

Kelly was smiling knowingly, as if she understood all too well. Her engagement ring, a flawless dazzling diamond, sparkled. "I hate to cut into your daydreaming time, but Spence wants to see you. Another tenant in the corner office is pulling out. Plus, Ava and Aubrey are really going at it. You might want to referee."

"My destiny in life." She didn't mind; she felt the pull of work and her responsibilities, but she couldn't seem to make her feet work. She was rooted in place, as if trying to hold on to a moment that had already passed. How could it be possible she missed Jack already? "I'll be right in."

Kelly didn't budge either. "Hayden seems pretty unhappy about this. Her glare factor has turned toxic. She's been staring poison at you."

Katherine nodded. She didn't know what to say. Jack had to know how his daughter felt. "And I was just starting to feel…" as if this was a dream in the making. "When I'm with him, it's as if I'm standing in the brightest sunshine. When he's gone, I'm alone in the dark."

"Sounds like the real thing to me." Kelly made her engagement ring sparkle again, just to admire it. "Sometimes I still can't believe this is real. It's like I'm waiting to wake up and realize falling in love with Mitch was just a dream."

"He's a good man, and you deserve to be cherished by him forever." Katherine's heart filled with sympathy and caring for her cousin. Kelly's road had once been difficult, too.

Kelly sighed, an utterly contented sound of happiness. "Do you know what someone said to me a while back? Good things happen to good people. Now I'm saying it to you. This will work out for your greatest good. I *know* it."

"I pray that's true." Katherine fell silent, keeping her fears inside.

Chapter Fifteen

The image of Katherine standing in front of the store, washed in sunshine, stayed with him like a beacon, guiding him and growing more radiant every time he thought of her.

"Dad, this is so bogus." Hayden slumped in her seat looking as sour as ever. "Thought I was done with this youth-group junk."

"What's with the attitude about the youth group?" Jack didn't get it. He eased the SUV through the icy lot, looking for parking. The place was packed. "You liked the youth group at our old church."

"That was before I had nothing in common with them."

Whatever lay behind that sounded like a long discussion to him, and they were running late as it was. He pulled into the fire lane alongside the curb. "We'll unload you, so you can meet Marin on time. Then we'll talk on the way home."

"More joy to look forward to." She rolled her eyes, released her seat belt and bolted out of the vehicle.

She was particularly sour today, as overcast and angry as the sky. Black clouds shoved at the mountain peaks, obscuring them. The wind had a vicious bite as he climbed out to fetch Hayden's skis from the roof rack.

She didn't seem thrilled when she took possession of them and leaned them against her shoulder. "You're going to meet *her* again."

He nodded. "I'm giving you time to get used to the idea. So it would be good for both of us if you did that before we head home tonight."

"The joy never ends." With that she stomped away.

He loved his little girl; not that she was so little anymore, but she would always be his little Hayden. Nothing could ever tarnish his commitment to her. He'd prayed hard and he was sure of his path. He wanted the best possible outcome for his daughter. And for himself.

He loved Katherine with such devotion for a reason. She couldn't have captured his heart unless she had a heart big enough to love Hayden, too. He knew she did. And that only made him love Katherine more. This would be the best thing for all of them, he was positive. As he drove around impatiently, looking for an available spot, he had plenty of time to think. To prepare.

While he and Katherine were only officially on date number two, they'd already been through a lot together. Enough for their initial affection to turn into something substantial. No, correct that. Into something rare. Such a strong stirring of love, soul-deep, could only be heaven sent. Meant to be.

Finally someone backed out of a spot and he slipped into it. Cut the engine. Pulled the brake. He was hardly aware of the vicious bite of the freezing air when he opened the door, or the slight slip of his boot on the ice when he stood. What he *did* feel was Katherine's presence like the air on his face. She was an awakening in his spirit that was pure destiny.

He didn't have to look around the crammed acre-wide parking lot to search for her. He turned toward her, finding her by feel. The brightness within his soul intensified when their gazes locked. She was waiting just beyond the entrance to the lodge, at the edge of the skiing area, looking amazing. When she smiled, it moved through him like grace.

His heartbeat thundered to a stop and he reached for her hand. Through layers of fabric, he could feel the weight of her hand, the shape, the warmth and the connection. Maybe it was more than physical touch, he realized. More like spirit touching spirit.

Words lost their meaning. He couldn't find a single way to say what he felt, and anything as mundane as "Hi," or "It's good to see you," fell far short of the experience of holding her hand, gazing into her eyes and seeing forever. Their forever.

Like a dream, he leaned forward, inexorably, moved by feeling and not thought. He watched Katherine's eyes grow wider, as if in surprise, and then she dipped her chin, shy, and gazed up at him through her lashes.

He knew that she felt this, too. Closer still he leaned, towering over her, slanting his mouth over hers. A hush filled him, soul-deep, and he brushed his lips to hers in a first, tentative kiss.

Time stood still, the world stopped turning, and it felt as if heaven watched, waiting. Jack was aware of Katherine's fingers tightening around his, and he felt the tides of her heart, her hope for his honest love, her dreams that were exactly his.

Perfection. He straightened slightly, breaking

their kiss just enough so he could look at her. Feel her smile. See her love for him in her eyes. Know that she felt this monumental change, too.

It was all there on her face, in her heart and soul. He cradled her chin in his free hand, thinking how precious she was, and wanting nothing more than to cherish her the way a husband cherished a wife. With all he was and all he had and all he would ever be.

She was blushing slightly, shy and demure, but she looked happy. "I was going to ask you where your skis are, but, wow, my mind is a complete blank."

But not your heart. He kissed her again.

No, not my heart, she thought, letting her eyelids drift shut, giving herself up to the sweetness of his kiss. More confident this time, she curled her fingers into his coat, holding on. Like sunlight warming all the shadows and hurt places, his kiss filled her with hope, with a perfect peace, with a love so bright she was blind to everything else but this man.

When he lifted his lips from hers, the bond of their hearts remained. This was definitely a sign, she thought as she let him gather her in his iron-strong arms and fold her against his chest. She sighed, resting against him, her heart full, and her soul brimming, no longer afraid to believe. She felt his kiss through the knit yarn of her ski cap.

"It's cold out here," he said.

"Is it cold? I hadn't noticed."

His chuckle rumbled through his chest and into her. "I was hoping to get you inside where it's warm. And where I can order some lunch before we hit the slopes. I didn't get a chance to eat."

"Sure." What she wanted was to stay like this forever, in his arms, against his heart and never let him go. As if he could sense her wish, he slid one arm around her shoulder, keeping her close, and took her hand in his free one, holding her as they walked side by side.

This is more than a dream, it's a prayer answered, Katherine thought as she practically floated down the sidewalk and into the lodge. She hadn't been this happy in forever.

"It's packed." Jack's words tickled her ear. "Let me go see if I can persuade the waitress to serve us in the extra dining room. Stay here where it's warm."

Only then did she realize she was standing in the radiant heat of the enormous fireplace, with skiers all around her. They were chattering over cups of tea or hot chocolate, warming up before going back out and making the most of the fresh powder.

Her happiness lifted a notch when she spotted Jack at the hostess's stand, talking with the manager. He looked good, solid, and he was hers. This all feels too good to be true, she thought, pulling off her gloves. But it is true. This is really happening.

Please, Lord, don't let this end.

"Katherine!" It was Lori Brisbane, a member of their church and a longtime bookstore customer, coming out of the gift shop. "It's wonderful to see you out of the store enjoying yourself. Did you know that Ava did my sister's wedding cake? Kristy was in tears she was so happy with it."

Katherine nodded, although she hadn't heard that bit of news. That Ava and her secrets. "Have you heard from Kristy?"

"Are you kidding? She's in Hawaii. She doesn't have time for her sister." Her smile was bright and joyful. "Although I'll be having a honeymoon of my own soon. I just got engaged."

"Congratulations. I thought I recognized that smile. The look of a happy woman."

"I notice you have that look, too." Lori winked as she backed away. "I've got to get back to Wade. Bye."

Jack. Katherine could feel his approach. She knew the way the air changed when he was near. The way her spirit turned toward him like the moon to the earth. The sight of him eclipsed all else.

His hand found hers and made her joy double. "Hi, beautiful. I see you're popular."

"Oh, that was Lori. Practically everyone from town seems to be here."

"It's supposed to rain up here by week's end. That'll be the end of skiing. I guess everyone's here for one last day. Good news. I secured a fairly quiet table for two."

"Romantic."

"That's the idea." Jack guided her through the crowded lobby and into the dining room. On the other side of another fireplace wall was a dining room the same as the one they'd been in before, except the tables were set and ready for customers.

One table, beside the fireplace and facing the windows, held menus, a steeping pot of tea and water glasses. He pulled out the chair that had the best view for Katherine. She brushed past him, sweet floral and vanilla fragrance, and the memory of their kiss heartened him. She poured the tea, his cup first.

He pushed the sugar jar in her direction.

"See how well this second date is going? I'm luckier on second dates. Usually there are fewer disasters."

"Wow. This means no meteorites will suddenly burn through the roof and strike our table?"

"Nope. There won't be a kitchen fire, an avalanche that wipes out the lodge, nothing on a personal level of disaster either. Like an old girlfriend walking into the dining room or someone I arrested accosting me while my back is turned. Those are all first-date disasters."

"I'm glad we're well past that. You never did finish telling me about the rest of your top worst. I suppose you just did?"

"Yep, but I'm all past that now. For good, I'm thinking." He laid his hand over hers.

His loving touch could erase any hurt. Make her forget the past.

That's when she saw the past walk into the dining room, in the wake of a busy, fast-walking waitress, and a pleasant-looking woman. Kevin, with his infant son in a baby carrier, tucked in beneath a blue blanket. Kevin, unaware of her yet, held the chair for his wife, much the same way Jack had held her chair moments ago. The woman smiled up at him adoringly as she settled into the chair. The moment Kevin set the little baby on the table, she checked on him. They were the picture of a perfect family.

I'm glad for him, she thought. Kevin wasn't the right man for her, but seeing him now felt like a slap to the face. A wake-up call. A sign.

No, it isn't a sign, she thought stubbornly. That was past. His rejection didn't hurt anymore. But Jack's would devastate her.

"Is something wrong?" Jack was studying her with concern. "You look as pale as a ghost."

"I'm all right. You know how you mentioned an old girlfriend showing up? Well, I almost married that man."

"Who, him?" Another waitress had bounded into the room, leading another couple to one of the tables.

"The other guy." She watched Jack twist to study the small family at the other side of the dining room. Kevin's back was to him, which was good. That meant he was looking in the opposite direction. "It's okay, I was over it long ago."

"He's the one who changed his mind, right?" Jack turned back around.

The waitress hurrying toward them to take their order saved her from having to answer. She swallowed hard, trying to tuck her emotions inside. The happiness she felt dimmed a little, and she could feel her shadows and fears.

Don't think about those, Katherine. She studied the menu and randomly picked something. Her pulse thudded in her head. Her palms were damp. She felt the shadows and fears deepen.

Jack isn't like Kevin, she reminded herself while Jack ordered and handed over his menu. The waitress hurried off. Katherine had no idea what Jack had ordered.

"I've given some thought to what you said."

She blinked. What had she said? Her mind was spinning. She couldn't remember, couldn't focus. There was Kevin in the background, sitting ramrod-straight, shoulders perfectly parallel to the floor, just like Jack. Every hair in place, just like Jack. Wearing a ski sweater and jeans ironed into wrinkle-free perfection. Just like Jack.

Jack took a swallow of tea. "I appreciate what you want to do for Hayden. I'll leave it up to you. If you want to hire her, then offer her a job. See what she says."

That surprised her. "That's okay? I guess I thought—" She let the sentence drift and added more sugar to her tea.

"You thought when I said I wanted Hayden to work for free, that nothing would change my mind, right?"

"It did occur to me."

"I get why you think that. I come on strong. It's a fault, and I try not to, but it happens. Like the afternoon we first met. I come across as it's my way or the highway, but I always listen to reason, eventually." He leaned closer, intimately, his voice dipping low, full of promise. "I'll always listen to you."

He cradled her hand, as if he thought her the most treasured woman in the world. But it was the way he was looking at her that made both terror and joy rip through the core of her spirit, with admiration, with respect, with all-out adoring love. This is what she saw in his heart, the kind of affection he held for her. More than anything she'd ever known before.

It was also terrifying because she'd passed the fail-safe point in this relationship and there was no turning back. Her heart was wide open, her love for him soul-deep. He'd peeled back every layer of defense she had simply by being in love with her, and she was helpless. Defenseless. That was the only way to love someone, but love was a risk. It came with no guarantees.

How had it happened? She'd fallen so hard in love with him she felt a piece of her deepest self crack in fear. Danielle's words kept burdening her, when they should have been reassuring. *If this guy isn't the kind of man to accept what happened to you, then he isn't good enough for you.*

The waitress arrived with their food, setting down her bowl of soup and his plate with a thick sandwich and a mountain of curly fries. Katherine bowed her head for the blessing, adding silently to Jack's prayer, *Lord, I put my trust in You, that You will help me. I need a sign. Give me a sign of whether I can trust him.*

So much of her was at risk, she couldn't hold down the terror. After the blessing, Jack withdrew his hand from hers and dug into his roast beef sandwich.

She could only stare at her steaming bowl of soup. There was a horrible sense of impending doom, like the finger of a tornado overhead, swirling and waiting, looking for the right moment to touch down.

You've given this to the Lord, remember, Katherine? She tried to relax. To stay calm. This was out of her hands. It was in God's.

And in Jack's.

"There's Hayden," he said, nodding toward the window.

Marin's teenagers were awkwardly trudging sideways on their skis up on the slope, along the crest of the small incline and down, out of sight. Katherine forced her voice to sound normal. "By this time next year, she'll be taking the advanced run by storm."

"You know it. She's also going to be happy again. And I owe it all you, Katherine."

She froze, feeling the wind shadow from that tornado overhead, like the first sign that her dreams were about to shatter.

Jack kept on going, confident, and his adoration quadrupled. It was in his words, in his gaze, in his touch as he reached across the small table and caught hold of her hand, and in the very air surrounding them. "None of this would be happening if you hadn't come into our lives. Hayden's turning a corner, I think. I was able to forgive Heidi when I didn't know I hadn't. You showed me that by your example, Katherine."

"You give me far too much credit. Please, Jack, don't—"

"You're modest, too. You have been a stellar role model for Hayden. You are a prayer answered for me. You're just…perfect."

Perfect. There was the tornado touching down, right in the middle of her heart. Shredding any chance, every chance at a lasting love with Jack. Pain splintered through her. *Perfect.* Why had he chosen that word? "J-Jack, you have n-no idea."

"I know that every hardship in the past few years, after losing Heidi nearly did me in. It's been tough. I didn't understand why at the time, but I see it now. I had to go through that to get to the other side. To be different, to be better. To be with someone as amazing as you."

"N-no, Jack." Stop him, she had to stop him, but she couldn't seem to make her tongue form the words she had to say. She had to tell him. Right now. Before he went one step farther and started talking about how she'd make the perfect wife and mother of their children.

"No, I want you to hear this." He was smiling, gazing down at her as if he thought her beyond compare, as perfect as he'd made her up to be.

As she'd let him believe because she hadn't told him. But it was too late now, she saw, as he lifted her left hand and leaned forward just enough to press his lips to her ring finger. Did he pick that finger intentionally? Agony sheared through her, and she pulled her hand away, wadded up the napkin in her lap and shoved off from the table.

He'd stood too, his forehead furrowed with concern, surprise on his face, love in his eyes.

He didn't understand. He would never understand. And she knew why, hearing his words, his voice, as fresh in her memory as when he'd said them over the phone after their first date. *I have to do what's best for my little girl, hands-down.*

Of course he did. Absolutely. But how was she going to be able to tell him the truth, when he was gazing at her as if she was his answered prayer? She was certainly far from that, and she knew, no, she *feared,* that if she opened her mouth and the truth spilled out about that horrible time that had nearly broken her spirit forever, he might sympathize. Maybe he'd be fairly understanding about it. Maybe he wouldn't be as harsh as Kevin had been in his rejection of her.

But it would come in a worse, more devastating way. His precious love for her would fade. The tenderness in his voice would vanish. And the way he looked at her—the way she treasured more than anything in her life— would wither away. She was scared that when he looked at her, he would see a woman not good enough to be a stepmother and influence on his teenage daughter. Someone he could not respect for a wife.

So, instead of his adoration, she would look into his warm, dark eyes and see disrespect. And imagining that cracked her into a thousand pieces, like the crater in the aftermath of a twister, nothing but scorched earth and devastation where life and hope used to be.

Tears blurred his handsome face, as she fought hard to find the right words to fix this. To salvage his regard for her.

But what? There were no words, no easy phrases, no way to lightly comment that not all first-date disasters were funny. That some were the exact opposite of what a date should be, with mutual respect and regard, with the hope for the first step to a great lasting love. That some were destructive and violent and cruel.

Maybe she'd simply walk away now because in the end, it would be the same. She would lose Jack eventually, as soon as he learned the truth. He wasn't the man she was searching for. He wouldn't understand. No matter how hard she'd prayed for him to be.

Why couldn't she have seen this coming? She could have realized this sooner, she knew how important his daughter was to him. That was one of the reasons she loved him so greatly. But it was a love that could not be.

"I'm sorry, Jack. I—" Blindly, she grabbed her coat and her bag and took off, choking back her tears, holding down her sobs, willing down the pain. Leaving him confused behind her, then running after her, but she beat him to the parking lot. She slid behind the shadow of a minivan, blocking her from his sight.

But he followed her anyway, tracking her through the icy parking lot. "Katherine? Are you all right? What's going on?"

Why did he have to be so caring? Didn't he know what he was doing to her? Ripping her to pieces a second time? She turned to face him when she wanted to run. She found words when she didn't know she had any left inside her. "I thought this was going to work, but it's just... not."

"I don't understand." He'd reared up like a startled bear looking around for the threat. "Is it that guy in the dining room? Did seeing him upset you?"

"No. This isn't going to work."

"We were in there having a meal and everything was fine. What happened? What upset you like this?"

Just tell him, Katherine. Tell him the truth.

That's what her heart was saying, but her mind—logically, she knew if she did, it would be a worse disaster than this.

She was minimizing the pain and the loss. That was the mistake she'd made with Kevin. She'd waited too long to tell him, trusting him when that trust had been misplaced. She wouldn't make that mistake again. And not when the love she felt for Jack was so strong, she could feel the confusion roiling inside him, the protective anger and confusion and, greatest of all, his love for her.

She took a step back, shivering, as the first flakes of snow fell, drifting from heaven like purity and goodness, like a brush of grace she couldn't let herself feel.

Jack swiped his hand to his forehead, as if he were trying to think, as if he were so upset it was an effort to stay calm and logical. "It was me. It was something I said. I was pushing you. I just have never..."

He shook his head, a big mountain of a man, looking helpless, open and vulnerable. All heart. "I've never felt this way before. So strongly before. So fast and one hundred percent. I just wanted to let you know what I think of you. That I'm committed. That I'm not like that lunkhead over there who changed his mind. I'm not that way. You know that, right?"

She was hurting him. That was the last thing she meant to do. She laid her hand on his, and the connection from her soul to his zinged through her like a rainbow across the sky. It wasn't real. As beautiful as it was, it was only an illusion.

And that's what this love between them had been. All it could ever be. She wanted Jack to be a man that he wasn't, the same way he wanted her to be a perfect example of what was good and right for his daughter.

"Goodbye, Jack." She held her chin high, determined to do this the right way. Dying inside, appearing calm on the outside took all her strength of will, but she did it. "I think you are an incredible man. I wish more than anything that this could have worked out. You deserve the woman you think I am."

She backed away, watching as the sky opened up and snow fell in a veil between them. Like a sign from heaven separating them. Hadn't she prayed for a sign? And God had answered that prayer.

This is for the best, she told herself as she hurried through the jam-packed lot. Car after car was empty and still, quickly blanketed by snow. No one was around, everyone was inside the lodge or skiing on the runs, and she felt the vast loneliness with every soundless footstep.

He never would have loved her anyway. Not enough.

She caught a blur of movement through the blur of the snowfall, at the edge of her vision. Jack, come after her? She wondered, turning instinctively toward him. But it was someone else heading toward the lodge. Jack was a faint shadow standing right where she'd left him, a perfect image with hands fisted, jaw set and powerful body braced as if ready to fight. Then he hung his head in defeat.

I'm so sorry, Jack. It was fear that drove her forward; loss that numbed her to her core. She was too cold inside to feel the icy needles of snow or wind on her face. She beeped her car door unlocked and dropped into the seat, finally alone, willing down tears. It never would have worked anyway, this is better, she told herself. There would only be more pain and hurt, more anger and bitterness. She knew that for a fact.

Her cell phone chimed and she dug in her purse for it. Stabbed it off without even seeing who was calling. It didn't matter. She didn't care. She'd lost Mr. Right, her soul mate, Jack who made her feel whole, who made the pain in her past fade away like shadows at high noon.

I had wanted him to be the one. She rested her face in her hands and gave in to the heart-ache.

Chapter Sixteen

On his way back to the table, Jack kept going over their conversation in his mind, especially what Katherine had said. *You deserve the woman you think I am.*

What did that mean? And what had he said to make her run out on him like that? He'd come on strong, that was it. He sent a glare across the dining room at the man who'd changed his mind about marrying Katherine.

How did anyone change his mind about Katherine? Jack didn't get it. Love wasn't about deciding who to marry; it was a power that came from down deep, a binding affection that had little to do with logic and everything to do with heart. The strongest forces in life were that way. Faith. Honor. Commitment. Integrity. Love for family. The need to protect and take care of them.

"Oh, good, you came back." The waitress hurried up to him. "I thought you'd run out on the bill. You'd be surprised how often that happens. Is there something I can do?"

"Box up the food for me." Hayden would probably snack on it later. As for him, he'd lost his appetite.

Was it over, just like that? He dropped back into his chair. He didn't know what to do. By the time he chased Katherine back to town, he'd have to turn right around and head up the mountain to pick up Hayden.

How could things do a complete one-eighty like that, just out of the blue? He remembered the look on her face, one of pure regret. Whole misery.

He looked over his shoulder. Katherine had had a clear view of her ex-fiancé and his wife and infant son all the while he'd been going on about how great she was and their future together.

On their second date. Maybe he'd pushed too hard. Maybe she was afraid of getting another proposal, and then having a man change his mind about her. That was not going to happen. He felt the dedication down to the underside of his soul. When God gave you a shot at a great blessing, a smart man didn't accept it with his brain, but his heart.

The question was, how did he fix this? How did he assure Katherine that he adored her, he was committed to her two thousand percent? That he thought she was beyond compare, and perfection on earth? How could he do all that to reassure her of his devotion and not scare her off?

He tried her cell again. Nothing. He called the bookstore. The cousin who was the cashier answered, the one who'd rung up his purchase yesterday. "Hi Kelly, have you heard from Katherine?"

"No. Isn't she there with you?"

"Not anymore. Can I leave a message for her to call me?"

It didn't seem like enough. He called her home phone. When her answering machine came on, and the gentle dulcet tones of her voice reached him, he felt the first hit of realization kick in. She'd called it off. She'd said it was wrong.

Maybe she'd meant he was wrong.

"Katherine." He fought to keep calm, to keep his mix of hurt and confusion and angst from turning into all-too-easy anger. "I'm sorry. I don't know what I did or what I said. Or if it's just me you think is wrong for you, but I'm asking you to call me."

He stopped short of saying too much. Like

"I love you. No, I don't just love you. It's like from here to the next galaxy and back. Big time, real love." He didn't know if that would scare her further or hurt her more. "Just...call."

He hung up and left his phone out where he could reach it fast if she should call. He didn't know what to do. He was stuck here until Hayden's group was done. Maybe, by the time he got her settled at home, he could run out and make sure Katherine got home safely. See if he could get her to talk.

See if there was a way to fix this.

The waitress returned with the soup in a container, his sandwich boxed and a new pot of tea.

This couldn't be happening. It just couldn't. He poured a cup of tea, feeling the steam rise against his face. The shock was starting to wear off, he could feel the heat from the steam and the chill from standing outside without a coat in a snowstorm. Desolation spread through him.

What if there wasn't a way to fix this? What if Katherine meant what she said, that it was wrong and she was done seeing him? He wasn't going to be okay. Not by a long shot.

He stared out the window watching the snowfall, preferring the numbness of shock to the pain of losing a dream like Katherine.

* * *

Katherine stumbled into her lonely kitchen, feeling her way through the dark. Turning on the light wasn't going to help her. She felt blind, deaf and numb inside. Paralyzed from the inside out. She dropped her keys on the tray by the back door, hung her coat on the wall hook, unlaced her boots and just walked. Without thought or direction. Completely shut down. Because if she felt anything, even the carpet beneath her feet, then everything might pour out, like a floodgate being opened, and the rush of pain would be too much.

Don't think about him. Don't think about anything.

She found herself in the living room, facing the drawn blinds over the bay windows. She sank onto the cushions, staring at nothing. Feeling nothing.

Images welled up, images she blinked hard against. Kevin gazing at his wife like the paragon she probably was, the paragon he'd wanted. How that was similar to what Jack wanted.

Stop remembering, Katherine. It's only going to hurt, and for what reason? The past can't be changed. Wrongs done to you cannot be undone. There's only now and moving forward. And moving forward meant leaving Jack behind. Just letting him go. And trusting that there had to be another man out there somewhere who wasn't looking for perfection. A paragon, as Kevin had told her he'd wanted when he'd proposed.

Had she known that Jack had been thinking this all along, then she never would have encouraged him. She never would have gone on that date with him. She would have politely turned him down, just like the copier guy. Just like she'd done with a handful of men over the years. The ones who'd looked as though they might not accept her if they knew.

Or, maybe, just maybe, she was the one at fault. She'd run tonight without telling Jack the truth. And what did that make her? Tears burned behind her eyes. A failure? A coward? A liar? She didn't want to be any of these things. She believed in facing life honestly and as straightforwardly as possible.

She was trying to protect her heart. That was all.

A knock rapped against her front door, jarring the silence. Jack. Her pulse jackhammered and she spun toward the door. No, she couldn't face him right now. She was just too vulnerable. Every protective layer needed to be put back in place first. Her calm, her faith, her polite veneer, so she could be sensible, predictable Katherine again. Back in her rut.

The phone rang. She didn't move. She sat like a shadow in the dark as the answering machine kicked on.

"Hey, Kath." It was Holly, her voice warm and gentle with understanding. "I'm standing in your walkway. I know you're home. There's wet tire tracks disappearing beneath your garage door. Can I come in? I want to make sure you're all right."

No. Yes. Katherine didn't know what she wanted, but she couldn't turn away one of her dearest friends. Especially when it was snowing so hard outside and Holly had come to comfort her. So she stumbled her way through the room, turned on the small foyer light and unlocked the front door.

Holly tumbled in, dripping melting snow. "Hi. When I was done with my delivery at the gift shop, I hunted you down, but no you. Just Jack sitting alone in the dining room."

"Jack was still there?" Katherine woodenly took Holly's coat and hung it up to dry. She tried to take comfort in the fact that he hadn't come after her. And not to read it as a sign that he hadn't bothered.

Holly rubbed her arms. "It's freezing in here. Let me just turn up the heat. Oh, and you're sitting in the dark." She disappeared around the corner, flipping on lights on her way to the thermostat. "I had wanted to swing by and make you introduce me to him, so I could grill this guy, you know, see what I think he was made of."

"Not necessary." Katherine crossed her arms in front of her heart, the only shield she could manage. "Let me put some tea water on."

"Forget tea." The heat clicked on with a whir of air from the floor vents, and Holly strolled into sight. "I'm here because I can guess what happened. Jack was alone at that table, and he stayed that way. You were supposed to be there with him, so obviously something happened. He looked like the world had ended."

For her, too, Katherine realized.

"You don't look much better. I can't believe that he pulled a Kevin on you. Marin really thought he was a good guy. That he had his heart in the right place. C'mon, come sit down. Tell me what happened."

"You've got it all wrong." Why did that rip her apart even more? "I called it off. It was all me. I thought if I did, then I'd be saving us both more hurt down the line. But I don't know, this hurts much worse than I thought it would."

"But you told him, right? Isn't that why you're in tears?"

Katherine shook her head, collapsing onto the corner of the coffee table. "I couldn't make myself say the words."

"Why not?" Kindness. Comfort. Friendship. Holly sat down across from her on the couch. "Was he mean?"

"That would have made it easier. Do you know what he said? He thinks I'm a stellar role model for Hayden. I'm a prayer answered. That I'm perfect." Katherine hid her face in her hands, bleeding from the soul. "He doesn't see me at all. He's imagined the woman he wants and has confused me with her. It's what Kevin did. He saw what he needed, not who I am. And it was so the opposite of what he'd decided I was, that when I finally told him the truth, he couldn't accept it. I hadn't been honest with him soon enough."

"That isn't something you tell any stranger up front."

"But a boyfriend? Someone I'm in love with? Yes, it is. But it doesn't matter now." She didn't have to open up that painful chapter in her life and go back over it. "Enough. I can't stand to think about this."

It was like going under for the third time,

knowing it was her last breath of air. Some things, even far in the past, hurt too much.

Holly was silent for a while and Katherine was grateful for that. It gave her time to battle down the sobs rising up in her throat. To will down the tatters of memories and the pieces of her heart. To lean on her faith and pray, asking for the strength to get through this the right way.

"Let me get this straight," Holly finally said. "You ended this because you thought he wouldn't understand? You rejected him because you *thought* that's what he was going to do to you?"

"It doesn't sound so good when you say it." She swiped at the pooling tears blurring her vision. "He's not going to think I'm such a fine example for his daughter if he knows."

"You don't know that. Besides, that doesn't make sense, Katherine. You didn't choose what happened to you."

"No, but not everyone understands that. Even my own father said at the time, 'How could you let that happen?'" She swiped her hands over her face, wanting to hide, wishing she could remove the pain and confusion by hitting a delete button. One click and it would be all gone. Impossible, she knew.

"Remember when I told you that love is

opening a door in your heart and letting that one other person in?"

Katherine nodded; she knew her friend meant well. "You said one of the hardest things is to love without defense. I know that's what you're going to say I didn't do. That I pushed him away, and I did, but not for that reason. He said—" She closed her eyes, knowing it was only half the truth. "I panicked. I don't want him to know what happened. I can take a lot of things, but I don't think I can stand having him look at me differently. I just…can't do it."

"You don't know what he would have said. Now you never will. What if you're wrong?"

She couldn't consider that right now. Not at all. She had to make a plan to get through the next few days. That meant life as usual tomorrow. Work, dinner with her sisters, maybe a stop on the way home past the nursery. The climbing roses she'd ordered last fall had come in. Back to her garden. Back to her friends. Right?

Then why did it feel so wrong?

Someone pounded at the door. Marin's voice penetrated the thick wood. "Hey, in there! Open up. I have chocolate ice cream and I'm not alone. Ava brought pie."

"The reinforcements have arrived," Holly rose. "I'll let them in."

* * *

"Dad, are you okay?"

Jack pretended he didn't hear Hayden over the rumble of the garage door closing. "Leave the skis. I'll worry about unloading later."

He grabbed the to-go bag the lodge's waitress had been kind enough to provide for him and sloshed through the snow tumbling off the sides of the SUV. He inserted the key, turned the bolt and led the way inside. After turning on lights, he dropped the bag of food on the kitchen counter and kept going.

No blinking light on the answering machine. No call on his cell. He scrolled through the received calls list to check and see if Katherine called but left no message. She hadn't.

There was a rustling of the bag behind him. "Hel*lo?* Are you going to answer me?"

That got his attention. "What?"

"Are you finally going to tell me the big mystery? I thought Katherine was going to be at the lodge and I had to be all polite an' stuff. She's not coming here, right?"

He shook his head, despair clogged in his throat, and he couldn't speak. Didn't trust himself to. There was nothing to say about Katherine. Nothing he wanted Hayden to know.

She opened one of the containers and then

checked out the soup. "I'm gonna take this to my room, 'kay? I gotta study."

Normally he was pretty strict about sit-down meals, but he didn't have the heart for trying to make conversation. Even with his daughter.

She marched upstairs and he waited until he heard the click of her door shutting before he reached for the phone. He punched in Katherine's home number and listened to it ring. The machine picked up. No message. He'd already left one.

Maybe she's home, monitoring her calls, and she doesn't want to talk to you, buddy. That was a distinct possibility. Maybe he'd zip over there and try to talk to her. Try to fix this before the sun went down.

Be real, Jack. There may be no way to fix this. Katherine had taken off on him. She'd been clear that she'd been wrong about them. If he thought about it much more, if he let this emotion settle, then devastation was going to take over. Take him down.

His pager vibrated. He wasn't supposed to be on call, but it didn't surprise him. The roads were a mess, the snowstorm in the mountains was working its way to the valley floor as the evening temperatures dropped. Black ice was everywhere.

Change of plans. He dialed up Mrs. Garcia,

and on his way down the hall, he told Hayden he had to go out. She looked immersed in her schoolwork. A textbook was open. Her computer monitor glowed next to her.

"Bye, Dad," she mumbled without looking up.

Something felt wrong. It was a hunch, that was all, but he couldn't put his finger on what was off. Probably it was his own turmoil that was behind it.

He closed his bedroom door and hauled out a uniform. On his way out the door, he took the sandwich and a few cans of soda. It was going to be a long night, he guessed, and he wouldn't get the chance to stop for a meal, much less for anything else. Dealing with Katherine would have to wait.

Chapter Seventeen

After closing and bolting her front door, Katherine watched out the living-room window to see that Marin made it to her car safely.

"I'm taking a pillow from your bed, one of the squishy ones." Ava ambled down the hallway in a pair of bright-pink flannel pajamas. "Aubrey wants you to know her electric blanket isn't working."

"I have a new one in the back of the guest bedroom closet," Katherine answered absently as she watched Marin open her car door and slip inside. "I wish she'd left earlier like Holly did or else stayed here with us."

"She'll be fine. She's a most excellent driver. Unlike me." Ava shrugged.

"You're just a disaster, sweetie." Katherine couldn't help the pang of adoration she had for her sister. Ava *was* a disaster, but she was the best and nicest disaster in the entire universe. "Does Aubrey need help changing the blanket?"

"Nope. She'll have to endure my assistance. Come back after you make sure Marin gets off and we'll say our prayers together, okay?"

"Sure." She listened to Ava pad off, and the muffled voices of the twins from the spare room, which held twin beds for just this sort of occasion. The merry chattering was a comforting sound, a living sound, chasing away all the echoing emptiness that so often filled her little home.

Thank you, Lord, for the precious blessings of my sisters and friends. Katherine's heart wrenched, as if grabbed by giant pliers and twisted hard. It wasn't right that one decision to go on one date fifteen years ago could haunt her still. Make her afraid to trust.

Holly had been right. Her friends had rallied around her, the twins had shown up for support, Danielle had called and even Spence had made a rare brief stop to make sure she was all right. They had all mistakenly assumed she'd told Jack about the worst year of her life, and he'd rejected her. That he'd pulled a Kevin on her.

She'd seen the sympathy for her in everyone's eyes. Even sadness and disappointment.

It was so hard for her to trust. Her illusions as an innocent, rose-colored-glasses college student had been shattered one cold night in November, along with her blind trust that a man would automatically respect a woman, value her and treat her accordingly.

Holly's question haunted her. *You don't know what he would have said. Now you never will. What if you're wrong?*

Don't think about that, Katherine. This was like any other guy she'd been briefly dating that hadn't worked out. No biggie, right?

Except for the tiny fact that she'd fallen irrevocably square in the middle of the point-of-no-return phase, and there was no going back. She could break up with Jack. Tell him it was over. Tell herself she needed to move on, but that didn't change the fact. She placed her hand over the wrenching agony in her heart. That's where he was, right here, his love an invincible light still burning. What about that?

Red lights flashed on the frosty window glass, catching Katherine's attention. Marin's sedan hesitated in the middle of the driveway, headlights flicked on to highlight the sheen of icy snow plastered everywhere, and then slowly she drove around the curve and out of sight.

"Katherine, help!" Ava hollered, her voice

echoing down the hall. "We've got the control thing all messed up."

"*You've* got it messed up," Aubrey admonished. "I'm doing just fine, if you would let go of it."

The twins were cheerfully arguing, as always. For some reason, the damn broke in Katherine's carefully controlled emotions. Up they welled, despite the fortifications of the bowls of chocolate ice cream and slices of fudge pie, despite the comfort and sympathy of her loved ones. How had Jack come to mean so much to her? Why did it have to be him who'd taken down the walls she'd spent the last fifteen years building?

Because he was the one. Her soul mate. And Holly was right. She'd blown it. She'd panicked and run because she thought he wouldn't love her unconditionally. Because she couldn't trust that he would.

The problem is with me, she thought. All me. I'm afraid to trust him with all my heart. Him accepting me or not is a separate fear.

"Katherine!" Ava called again. "Make her stop!"

She twisted away from the window. "You sound like you're three years old. Kindergarteners behave better than you two."

"Hey, we were never well-behaved kinder-garteners." Ava laughed at something that had happened in the room. "Oops!"

Ava said that a lot. Katherine leaned one shoulder against the doorframe, taking in the chaos of one of the twin beds that had been so tidy ten minutes before. Ava had fallen hard onto her backside, her feet up in the air and the remote and cord to the blanket in her hands.

Aubrey snatched it out of her grip. "You are impossible. You're a burden to me. If I could, I'd auction you off."

"There'd be no takers." Ava pulled herself to her feet. "I have this reputation. It's why I can't get dates."

"Then we'll never be able to marry you off. How sad is that?" Aubrey knelt down and managed to stick the plug into the prongs at the hem of the blanket. "See? I told you it was simple. But you had to go and make a disaster of it."

"What can I say? I'm gifted."

Tears stung Katherine's eyes and burned in the back of her throat. Oh, she loved her sisters. Their funny, loving ways were exactly what she needed to get through the dark hours of the night. To help her pretend that she hadn't lost the best thing that had ever happened to her.

And it was all her fault. Her fault, and no one else's.

"There, it's put back together." Aubrey rolled her eyes. "Notice how your bed is neat and perfect and mine is the wreck?"

"I was just trying to help." Ava looked around, scanning the room. "I remembered to bring my Bible, but it's in my bag. O-okay, where did my bag go? I left it somewhere. But where?"

"We'll use mine." As if greatly burdened, Aubrey pulled hers off the nightstand. "Come sit down, Kath. If Ava hasn't scared you off."

"I'm fearless. I grew up with you two, remember?" Katherine eased back into the hallway. "I'll get my Bible and be right—"

The phone rang, startlingly loud in the late-night hush. Her first thought was Jack, and she froze. The phone rang again, and her second thought was Marin. The roads weren't good, and what if she'd had an accident? Katherine dashed for the nearest extension in her room before the answering machine could kick in.

The ID screen said it was from a pay phone. Nerves jerked into her stomach. What if Marin was hurt? "Hello?"

"K-Katherine?" It was a girl's voice that sounded small and unfamiliar and broken, as if she were crying. "Uh…this is Hayden. You know, Hayden Munroe."

Adrenaline shot through her system. Images of everything that could go wrong flashed through her brain in a single nanosecond. Jack shot on duty. A car accident. A robbery. A sudden medical problem. "What's wrong?"

A watery sniff. "C-could you come a-and g-get me?"

Get her? Wasn't she supposed to be at home or something? The bedside clock said it was ten minutes to eleven. Katherine's heart broke at Hayden's wrenching sob. A sound of genuine pain. "Sure. Where are you?"

"H-Hawthorne and White."

"What happened, is your dad there?"

"N-no. You g-gotta h-hur-ry." Harder crying. Utter misery.

"Are you hurt? Do you need an ambulance?"

"I'm o-okay. J-just c-come. *Please?*"

"Stay on the phone, okay? I'm going to give you to my sister. Aubrey!" She called down the hall. "Come take this and keep her on the line." She covered the mouthpiece. "Ava, get your cell and start calling around for Jack. The numbers I have for him are in my address book in the desk with the bills. Aubrey, find out for sure if she's in trouble and call 911 if she needs it. I'm going out." She talked into the receiver. "Hayden? I'm leaving right now, so talk to my sister until I get there."

"H-h-hur-ry."

"I promise." Katherine shoved the receiver at Aubrey and grabbed her purse on the way out the door. She couldn't bear to think what was wrong, what had happened to Hayden, but she knew firsthand the sound of serious pain. Of hurt and broken trust and betrayal.

She was out of the garage before the door had opened all the way, skating under it by a scant inch. Ice was everywhere, coating the driveway that had already been carefully treated by the management. She couldn't imagine how bad the city roads were. Snow hadn't been forecast for the valley, but the wintry mix of snow, sleet and ice was freezing upon contact. Her tires skidded when she turned toward the exit, and she was going only a few miles an hour.

Hawthorne and White wasn't far, but it would take forever for her to get there. She eased to a stop at the end of the driveway, but the tires couldn't get a grip. Luckily no traffic was coming on the main street, so she turned into the skid, kept the car going, and made the turn.

Please, Lord, watch over her until I can get

to her. Keep her safe. Katherine didn't know if her prayer could rise at all above the hard downbeat of the ice and snow. Anything could have happened to Hayden on a night like this.

Where was Jack? And why wasn't he with his daughter? More questions ate at her as she slid through intersections and up inclines toward the outskirts of town where the foothills, only a few hundred feet higher than the valley floor, were coated in snow as if a blizzard had hit.

Her studded snow tires should have been adequate, but they weren't. All she could do was pray with each slip and slide, each skid around a curve, that she'd stay on the road. She had to get to Hayden. She prayed harder when she met a car on the road, having the same difficult time keeping in its lane.

The snow flew dizzily at her windshield, knocked aside by the wipers. The constant whap, whap, whap knelled like seconds ticking by. She felt as if she were taking too long, running out of time. *Please, let Ava find Jack.* Maybe the state patrol was on its way.

Suddenly she saw the street sign. White. She was at the intersection on a stretch of country highway that led to the upper-class homes northeast of the city. Hawthorne shouldn't be too far. She slowed down, grateful that she was the only car on the road, looking for…she didn't know what she'd find.

She squinted through the thickening snowfall. There was the haze of a streetlight hovering ahead, growing stronger, giving way to a street corner with a small strip mall. A gas station and convenience store's outside floodlights glazed the ice and snow with an eerie gleam. There, against the night-dark parking lot, was a phone booth, wedged between the store and another building, dark except for a single security light.

Panic ratcheted through her. Hayden had called her from here. Where was she? Katherine slowed down, leaning over her steering wheel, squinting for any sign of anyone.

A shadow moved in the darkness and there was Hayden, in the narrow cut of the headlights, white with snow, bedraggled and dark with… blood. It stained the front of her ripped jacket.

Katherine was out of the car before she remembered stopping. "Hayden, what happened? You're hurt."

Hayden just stood there, tears rolling down her face, her voice high, near hysteria. "I'm so glad you came. Your sister said you were c-coming, but what if you cr-crashed, too."

Crash. "Were you in a car accident?" When Hayden nodded, Katherine felt fear shear through her soul. "Where's your dad? Was he driving? Was anyone else hurt?"

"N-no. He's at work-k." Hayden sobbed. "He l-left and then J-Jan and her boy-f-friend c-came by a-and—"

"You need an ambulance. Why didn't you call 911?" Katherine led Hayden to the passenger side and opened the front door. "We have to get you warm, and let me look. You have blood on you. We're going to need to call for help—"

"No! I'm not hurt. Dad c-can't know!" Terror paled her stark face. "Please. You have to help me."

"I will, Hayden. But you're hurt."

"It was a nose bleed, that's all. I swear. It's s-stopped n-now."

"Did you tell my sister about this?"

"A l-little."

"Good." That meant help was on the way. Aubrey would have made sure of it. The overhead dome light showed no wound, only a faint trail of dried blood above Hayden's upper lip. She was scared and cold.

Katherine reached for a blanket she kept beneath the seat. She shook it open and wrapped it around the girl. She seemed so young, so small. Katherine couldn't help the fondness rising up. "Is that a little better?"

Hayden's teeth were chattering, but she managed to nod. "K-Katherine? You c-can't tell anyone, okay? *Please?*"

"You know I can't do that."

"Yes, you can. You could take me h-home and Dad would never have to know. I'd work more hours at the store to make up for it. Not hours, weeks. Weeks and weeks."

"I'm not someone who can deceive your dad like that." She said the words gently, because she remembered what it had been like to be a teenager, but firm enough so there was no doubt. "You could have been seriously hurt tonight. You've been sneaking out on him all along, haven't you? That's not right, and it's not safe."

That's when she heard the faint scream of a siren above the rush of the storm. Jack. Katherine knew it even before she recognized the colors of a state patrol cruiser roaring their way, because of the shadows turning to light within her like a sun rising.

The cruiser skidded expertly alongside them and the door popped open. Katherine was already stepping aside, making way for Jack as he charged toward his injured daughter.

"Daddy!" Hayden's cry was both pain and relief.

The blue-and-red flash of an ambulance sliced through the thick snowfall, lumbering closer.

Katherine stepped back, into the darkness, into the protective veil of the storm. It was right that Jack was with Hayden, looking her over and then moving to the side to let the EMTs check her vitals.

The ghost of a memory haunted her, of her own father when she'd called him from the emergency room, alone, so utterly alone. And how he'd driven straight through the night to make it to Seattle. She hadn't been discharged yet, she'd had a broken wrist that had needed stabilizing and some lacerations. She could still see her daddy rushing through the hospital door, her stepmom a pace behind, terror and concern and love all tangled up as they wrapped her in an iron-strong hug.

I've come full circle. Somehow the old, haunting agony left her and she knew, somehow, that it was over. If she hadn't gone through what she had so long ago, then she wouldn't have been here to help Jack help Hayden. God had taken a horrible wrong in her life and made good of it in someone else's.

She no longer saw the teenaged girl, almost the age of the daughter she'd given away that sad, heartbreaking summer. Or felt the shock of whole innocence shattering that previous rainy November night on the university campus.

Maybe this was why Jack had been brought into her life. To heal them both, and to help Hayden when she really needed it. Maybe that had been God's true design, and the falling in love with Jack, that was her own doing.

As soon as the EMTs loaded Hayden into the back of the ambulance, she emerged from the night. She closed the passenger door and circled around to her side of the car. As she folded herself behind the wheel, she caught Jack's gaze through the swiping windshield wipers.

For one brief moment, they connected. The cold, the storm, the fear and worry, the sirens strobing faded into nothing but the beat of his gratitude. She nodded, all hope shattered, and drove out of the lot. That was the last she would ever see of Jack Munroe.

Chapter Eighteen

The hospital parking lot was packed on a night like this. Ice crisped every surface of the car. While the defroster wasn't making a dent, his wrath might. Jack had been terrified for Hayden, he'd hurt for her, he'd gone through the worst of all agonizing fear when he'd gotten Katherine's sister's call. It coalesced into red-hazed rage the instant he got her into the car. "What were you thinking?" he demanded.

"It wasn't all that bad. I don't have any broken bones."

The top of his skull was going to blow right off. "Do you know what I was doing when Katherine's sister called me?"

"She wasn't supposed to call you."

"I just finished helping with a family whose car had slid on black ice and hit a utility pole.

The father, who was driving, was seriously injured and so was his teenaged girl, who is your age. Even though she was wearing a seat belt, she hit her head so hard she didn't regain consciousness."

Hayden looked down, contrite. "I'm sorry."

"That could have happened to you. What were you doing in Jan's boyfriend's car?"

"R-riding."

"Racing?" He'd gotten the call from a colleague, who'd found the car in a ditch. Some kids this time of year raced on the slick country roads, spinning for kicks on the ice. There had been telltale skid marks. "I checked on the status of the girl from the accident while I was waiting for you. She has a hairline skull fracture, but she should be okay. She's lucky. That could have happened to you."

"Chill, Dad. Nothing happened." False bravado.

She just didn't get it. "Hayden, you deceived Mrs. Garcia. You lied about being in your room. You betrayed her trust and mine the second you snuck out your window. You put your safety and your life in danger."

"N-nothing happened." Her chin was trembling.

A crack in her shield. "This time. What about

next time? Maybe you'll break a bone. You could have been killed. I don't get this, Hayden. That's what happened to your mom."

"D-dad." Sheer pain echoed between them.

"And going off with Jan and her boyfriend. I don't know this kid. There was another car involved. Who was driving that car? Why did they leave you beside the road? It's a tough world out there and anything could have happened. You haven't seen what some people are capable of. You could've been assaulted or raped." He was blind with protective fury and heartbreak. He scrubbed his face with his hands. He shattered at the thought of his daughter hurt beyond repair. Hurt even more with a wound too deep to heal completely.

That thought troubled him. It had something to do with Katherine. But what? He heard the echo of her words. *It's not so much that you erase the wound from your heart, but that you learn to move past it.* He'd wondered over and over again how she'd become so wise in healing from deep pain. Maybe she'd been speaking of more than her mother's abandonment. Maybe much more.

"I—I'm sorry, Daddy." Hayden's voice seemed to come from far away. She'd put her face in her hands, muffling her words. "I don't know what's wrong. I hurt so much and it won't stop."

"Everyone has tragedy in their lives. It's a part of living. But you don't want to add to it, sweetheart. You can't erase the pain. You can't escape from it. Is that what you're trying to do?"

"I just—" She shrugged. "I don't know what's wrong with me. It hurts too much to keep pretending like everything's j-just peachy when it's not."

"No, it's not." He didn't think anything could hurt as much as seeing his daughter still in pain. But he was wrong. It was realizing how close he'd come to losing her forever. Realizing that anything could happen in the blink of an eye. "One wrong decision, one injustice, and life is never the same."

Jack hesitated, feeling an odd reminder. Katherine had said something about that. He had a hunch. A gut instinct. "Nothing bad happened this time, but that's not always going to be the case. You have enough pain, you don't want to bring any more hurt into your life. It's hard enough learning to live with the pain we have. To keep living in spite of it."

She sniffled, tears rolling down her face.

Yeah, him, too. "Do you know how much I

love you? Do you know what I went through after I got Ava's call?"

She shook her head.

"It was pure hell. It nearly destroyed me. What would I do if I lost you? You're my daughter. You are endlessly precious to me. I loved you from before you were born and there is nothing that will ever change that. You can test me, push at me with all you're worth, but you'll fail every time. I'm not going anywhere. I'm right here to help you through this."

She wrapped her arms around her middle, holding in so much pain. As if holding on. "You aren't gonna marry Katherine and forget mom, are you? Or me?"

"How could I forget you? You're half my heart, baby. And every time I look at you, I see your mom. There's no forgetting her. I promise you. We won't let that happen. I'll be grateful to her for you every single day for the rest of my life." He felt the truth in his soul. "Are we good? Are we going to get through this together?"

Hayden nodded, bowing her head. The sleet beat against the windows, blurring the outside world, letting in only the faintest of ambient light, but Jack had never seen so clearly.

They were going to be all right. All three of them. Hayden, Katherine and him.

God had led them here, intersecting their lives, finding for them the kind of love to heal the pain. That's what this bleak night was about. Jack was far from the most sensitive guy in Montana and he might not be the brightest bulb in the box, but he knew one thing. He loved his daughter. He'd never stop fighting for her. It would take time with Hayden, and he was committed all the way.

And if tonight hadn't happened, if he hadn't had time to sit in the emergency room and hear the sounds of other people's tragedies through the thin walls and not-so-private curtains, it wouldn't have gotten him to thinking. If Hayden hadn't jeopardized her safety and her life tonight, he never would have put it together. It was a cop's hunch, but he was right more often than not.

Katherine was wrong. She was the right woman for him. She was the only woman. He loved her without condition and without end. He'd do whatever he had to do to fix this. He'd show Katherine he was the right man, her man, and he was committed to her, one thousand percent.

Jack fastened his seat belt. "Let's get you home. You have some apologizing to do."

"To Mrs. Garcia?" She gulped. "To Katherine. She came and got me. When she didn't have to because I was real mean to her. I didn't know who else to call, but she came. And she was n-nice to me. And it wasn't because she likes you. She was just…nice."

"I know." He heard what she didn't say. He dug the ice scraper from beneath the seat. He kissed her brow, thankful she was here, unharmed, and grateful for the soul-deep feeling in his chest that told him they'd turned a corner. As tough as it had been, things were looking up.

He braved the icy storm and got to work clearing the windows. Maybe it was his imagination, but the stubborn winter winds didn't seem as brutal. As if everything, not just his luck, was changing for the better.

The sense of loneliness persisted in Katherine's condo, even with the twins asleep down the hall. As she roamed to the kitchen to reheat her cup of chamomile tea gone cold, she couldn't remember the place feeling so empty. So filled with shadows. So alone.

As she waited for the microwave to heat the tea, she had to be honest. She felt lonely. She felt empty. She felt shadows filling her up. Maybe that's what happened when you failed at what mattered most. Running away from true love instead of turning toward it. Isn't that what the Bible taught? That love was the greatest of all things, love gave worth and value and meaning to life. Maybe it was God's purpose for everyone on earth, including her.

How long had she been hiding behind the pain of what happened to her one November evening? She hadn't even realized it until she'd watched Jack and Hayden together, father and daughter, protective parent and trusting child. Somehow the ghosts of her past had been laid to rest and now there were no haunting memories to hide behind and no rationale to all that she'd been evading. She'd been horribly hurt long ago, there was no changing it, and some wounds to the spirit never fully healed. She had learned to live again but not to wholly love.

Had she chosen to date Kevin because he was a man who hadn't demanded emotional closeness? Kevin hadn't brought up all the feelings and shadows that being with Jack did. Kevin had felt placid and kind and comfortable. Jack was not.

Jack seemed to be able to see her soul, brightness and shadows. And he might not have pushed her when she'd evaded his personal questions about the emotional wounds in her life, but he'd felt them. Why did it terrify her to be so close to a wonderful, good man? Why did it feel as if she were about to jump out of an airplane without a parachute? A long free fall and then a fatal impact were certain. That's how it felt.

That's how it felt to think about trusting Jack wholly. No holds barred.

The microwave beeped, and she opened the door. Steam rose from the nearly full cup. Absently she wandered back into the living room. In the corner on the end table, a small red light flashed furiously. Her answering machine. Jack's messages. She hadn't listened to them and hadn't intended to. It would be safer to avoid them.

I asked God for a sign, and I got one. Jack wants a perfect woman for his daughter. That's what this is about. He's right, his daughter comes first, she thought as she cozied up into a big, overstuffed chair. Just forget it.

She set her cup on a coaster on the end table. The blinking answering machine light was like a signal beacon in the dark. *Look this way.*

She turned her back, settled into the corner of her chair, curled up her legs and opened her book. Just read, Katherine. Try to unwind. It's one in the morning and you've got to get to sleep. There's church in a few hours. She focused on the words on the page and nothing happened. They were just letters clumped together and seemed to make no connection in her brain.

She couldn't see the light, but she could *feel* it flashing. Insistent. Nagging, like her conscience. Whispering, like the inner voice she kept a deaf ear to because it was safer.

What do I do, Lord? She closed her book and bowed her head, frazzled, feeling as exposed as the jagged edges of shattered glass. *I'm too afraid to let this go. I'm too afraid to try to mend it. Maybe You could send a bigger sign, so I know. One I can't miss.*

Her biggest problem was that God could drop a twenty-foot neon sign on the carpet right in front of her, and if she didn't have her eyes open to see it, then what good would it do?

The emptiness within her ached like a broken bone. She couldn't take it anymore. She twisted around and hit the play button. The machine whirred and beeped. At the first sound of Jack's mellow baritone, the hurt inside her eased. Sweet longing filled her simply from hearing his voice.

"I'm sorry. I don't know what I did or what

I said. Or if it's just me you think is wrong for you, but I'm asking you to call me. Just…call."

She heard his raw misery. She buried her face in her hands, hearing with her ears and feeling with her soul. She'd hurt him deeply, the same way she'd hurt herself.

And now with the echo of his voice in the shadowed corners of the room, resounding in the empty chamber in her heart, she did not hide from the truth. She'd never felt a bond so strong. That nearness, the suggestion of his pain, that love for him shone inside her like a sun at full zenith. What more of a sign did she need?

Her words to Jack, spoken what seemed like so long ago now, came back to her. *I don't know if I just can't let go of controlling my life, or if I can't trust even God that much.*

What did that say about her faith? About her heart? She had constructed far too many shields to keep out the wrong things. A whole faith. A completing love. Belief that she could let go of trying to manage everything and it would still come out all right. Maybe better. Maybe much better.

Twin beams of light cut across the closed window blinds and disappeared. Odd, because the direction of traffic through the parking lot didn't usually send light into her front window. Was that the rumble of an idling engine?

Jack. It wasn't a thought; it was knowledge. She was peering through the slats in the blind, unaware what she was doing until she spotted a broad-shouldered hulk of a man behind the wheel of a state patrol car. The light shining within her quadrupled at the sight of him. Talk about a sign.

He looked up and his gaze fastened on hers. Across the distance, the night, the uncertainty and hurt, she felt his love. A rare, shining devotion that nothing—not even her fears—could break. As he climbed out of his car and strode down her walkway as committed as a soldier on a mission, she felt the strum of his heart within hers.

Somehow she had the doorknob in hand, the door was open. She didn't feel the cold sleet hammering against her or the merciless night wind. All she saw, all there was, was Jack.

Taking her in his arms, he pulled her flush to his chest, cradling her against his tender strength and steel. Right where she belonged. She felt his kiss against her temple and one big hand cradled the back of her neck, holding her as if cherished. It was pure heaven.

He whispered against her ear. "I already know what you can't say to me."

"What?" Who told? Ava, she was horrible at minding her own business. Tears welled up from those dark, soul-deep shadows.

Then it hit her. He knows. He knows and he's still here. He still loved her. Sobs broke free and she finally let herself relax into his embrace, into his comfort, into his love. Pure paradise.

"I put it together," he confessed. "From different things you said."

Wait a minute. He couldn't have put *everything* together. He didn't know the whole story. Her heart stopped. Her brain screeched to a halt. She felt her dreams fall like rain to the ground at her feet. She squeezed her eyes shut, vowing to savor the wondrous experience of being held in his arms even as she gently broke away from him. It was like turning down heaven.

"I've seen too much. I've been a lawman for sixteen years. I know what happens in this world. It wasn't such a stretch to put it together, Katherine. You were raped, weren't you?" He towered over her, his hand reaching for hers, to stop her from withdrawing, the precious love he had for her a certainty. It brightened the air around them and felt like hope on angel's wings. Far too precious a love to lose.

Katherine swiped the tears from her face and fought down the burn of defeat building in her chest. Whatever she did, she would not cry when she told him the rest of the truth. For there was another piece he could not have figured out on his own from anything she could have possibly said.

Lord, I hope I can find the words and the courage to do this. She was going to trust that she would not fall. She put her faith in Jack, the good man that he was, that he wouldn't pull away. A big risk. The hardest she had ever faced.

She had to prepare herself for him to turn away. After this, he would never see her the same way. It felt like dying simply to clear the emotions jammed in her throat. To look him in the eye. To face what was to come. To lose forever this moment between them. But the only thing worse than having him reject her would be to turn away from him now and live the rest of her life knowing she'd lost the best thing that ever happened to her because she was afraid.

She took a deep breath and just said it. "I was date-raped when I was a college freshman. I was seventeen years old. Two years older than Hayden. But there's more, Jack. Much more."

He waited, patiently, unwavering. She loved him the more for it, that he had no problem understanding that this had happened to her. She could see it on his face, feel it in her heart, that she didn't need to say how hard she'd fought, but she hadn't been strong enough to protect herself from a man almost twice her size and weight.

"If only this were the whole story. What I would give for it to be." She braced herself. He was going to withdraw now. This was where Kevin had lost it. She couldn't bring herself to say the words.

You've put this in God's hands, remember? Come what may, it is the right thing. She took a shaky breath, facing this man who waited so patiently, concern lining his granite features and his heart wide open.

"I, uh…" She paused, pressed her fingers to her forehead. There were no words to explain it. There was nothing left but the truth. "Nine months later I gave a baby girl up for adoption. Danielle came and stayed with me through the last trimester, so I didn't have to go through that alone. I—"

"You what?" Jack's eyebrows drew together as if he hadn't heard her right. As if he didn't understand. As if he couldn't quite believe what she'd said. "You went through with the pregnancy and gave a child away?"

That wasn't quite how Kevin had taken it. He'd have to get over the shock before he started ranting. So it was self-preservation that made her take a step back and turn away.

"How could you do that?" he asked.

Hold it together, Katherine. Whatever he says, you know the truth. How hard it was to go through. How it would always hurt. She carefully unlocked the deadbolt and pushed open the door. A silent invitation for him to leave.

When she turned around, there were tears pooled in his eyes. They did not fall, and after he blinked them back, she could almost fool herself into thinking she'd imagined it. He stood there, six feet three inches of pure gold, looking like a bear about to roar and attack.

"I can't believe you." He finally said, fisting his hands tight and then relaxing them. "I thought you were perfect before, but I was wrong."

See, he hadn't understood. But at least she'd done the right thing. This heartbreak had been worth the risk, she thought. Maybe it would be easier next time, *if* she ever dated to the point-of-no-return stage again.

Losing Jack this time meant that a part of her was never going to be the same. It was as if all the light in her faded into ultimate shadow.

He stalked forward, toward the door. No, toward her. He laid both big hands on either side of her face, cradling her tenderly. "You're even more perfect now."

He kissed her, ardent and tender so there was no doubt. A perfect hope lifted within her that outshone every fear. In the protective light of his love, she felt so radiant there was no dark place for a single shadow. Only joy.

When Jack broke the kiss, he didn't move away, didn't let her go. He would never let her go. Did she have any idea how amazing he thought she was? She was a woman who could love and live despite a terrible tragedy. "I didn't think it was possible to love anyone so much. And now you've gone and made me love you even more."

"That's exactly how I love you."

He could measure the truth of her words by the blazing brightness in his soul. By how she looked at him as if he were ten feet tall. Jack wiped the tears from her eyes with the pads of his thumbs. The love he had for this woman was endless. Infinite. She took everything and made it better. Tragedy. Mishaps. Happiness.

She'd even won over Hayden. She made him believe again in true love and heaven on earth.

This, he knew, was the beginning of real happiness. He saw his future roll out in front of them. Hayden doing well, graduating from high school, going on to college. Maybe more children to come. A happy marriage that was stronger every day. And all because of this woman who loved him. "How do you feel about a proposal on the third date? It's not too early?"

"I think it would be perfect timing." Her smile beamed joy.

"Then I can expect a yes to my upcoming proposal?"

"I predict a one-hundred-percent chance of it." Katherine couldn't believe it. But she felt the truth as he cupped her face in both of his big, tender hands. Oh, how she loved this man. With all her being. He was the right man for her. Heaven had been sending signs all along. She'd finally learned to listen.

Her soul stirred as he slanted his mouth over hers. His kiss was pure tenderness. Honest devotion. Respectful and sweet and full of promise. His love made her whole and hopeful, and that outshone every fear.

Thunder crashed overhead and wind gusted

against the side of the house. The Chinook wind turning the snow and sleet into rain. The warm sound hammered on the roof above them and drummed on the frozen ground outside, a sign that spring had come late, but that it had arrived.

The slightest pad of footsteps rustled in the hallway. There was no mistaking Ava's low whisper. "Uh-oh. I guess this means she's in her happily-ever-after stage."

"Finally," Aubrey whispered back.

Katherine broke the kiss and looked into her future husband's eyes. He was silently laughing, beaming with the same pure joy that she felt.

"Happily ever after," he whispered, folding her against his chest. "I like the sound of it."

"Me, too." She closed her eyes and listened to the steady, reliable beat of his heart.

* * * * *

Watch for Jillian Hart's
next Inspirational romance,
EVERY KIND OF HEAVEN,
available March 2007

Dear Reader,

Thank you so much for choosing *Precious Blessings*. I hope you enjoyed Katherine's story as much as I did writing it. Katherine has weathered a lot of difficulty in her life and hasn't let it embitter her or close her heart. I wrote this story because I wanted to remind others that no matter what storm you are weathering in your life, don't give up hope. Treasure all the precious blessings in your life and keep hope for all the wonderful blessings yet to come.

Wishing you peace, goodness and all of God's precious blessings,

Jillian Hart

QUESTIONS FOR DISCUSSION

1. What does Katherine first see in Jack that impresses her? What inaccurate first impression does she take away from meeting him? How does her second impression of Jack change her feelings toward him?

2. As Katherine gets to know Jack more, what aspects of his character does she come to admire?

3. A terrible wrong was committed against Katherine earlier in her life. How important was compassion from others in helping her through that hard time? Why?

4. Along the same lines, how does compassion from others help her in her life today? How is that demonstrated? How have you helped friends with painful past experiences?

5. How does Katherine take what she learns from a terrible hardship and make good from the bad? What impact does that have on the lives of the characters in the story? On Jack? On his daughter?

6. How does Jack's experience in life prepare him to be compassionate to Katherine's hardships? How does he show her that the real kind of love that the Bible teaches us is compassionate and selfless and larger than one person?

7. How is the importance of compassion and forgiveness demonstrated in this story?